Always a Fake Bridesmaid

CARRIE ANN RYAN
NEW YORK TIMES BESTSELLING AUTHOR

always a fake bridesmaid

A CLOVER LAKE / MONTGOMERY INK LEGACY CROSSOVER ROMANCE

CLOVER LAKE

BOOK 1

CARRIE ANN RYAN

Always a Fake Bridesmaid
By: Carrie Ann Ryan
© 2024 Carrie Ann Ryan

Cover Art by Sweet N Spicy Designs

This book is a work of fiction. Names, characters, places, and incidents either are products of the author's imagination or are used fictitiously. Any resemblance to actual events, locales or persons, living or dead, is entirely coincidental.
No part of this book can be reproduced in any form or by electronic or mechanical means including information storage and retrieval systems, without the express written permission of the author. The only exception is by a reviewer who may quote short excerpts in a review.

All content warnings are listed on the book page for this book on my website.

NO AI TRAINING: Without in any way limiting the author's [and publisher's] exclusive rights under copyright, any use of this publication to "train" generative artificial intelligence (AI) technologies to generate text is expressly prohibited. The author reserves all rights to license uses of this work for generative AI training and development of machine learning language models.

For Brandi.
I really blame you for this.
But Ewan thanks you.

always a fake bridesmaid

The moment Ewan McBride entered my life, my world tilted on its axis.

When we part, I promise him I owe him anything for saving my daughter's life.

What I didn't expect?

Being his fake date to a wedding—in two days.

It was only supposed to be a favor, but we can't deny the attraction.

Only he lives a state away and my life is in Colorado with my daughter and the Montgomerys.

This can only be one night that feels all too real.

Yet I know walking away will be the hardest thing I ever do.

**Always a Fake Bridesmaid is a next generation, single mom, grumpy rancher, fake dating romance set in the Montgomery World & Clover Lake series featuring Livvy & Ewan. Each book can be read as a complete standalone. An HEA is guaranteed!

Livvy Montgomery is Shep and Shea's daughter from Ink Inspired.

LIVVY

"MOM! Mom! Let me show you! Mom! Mommy! Mommy!"

As the dulcet tones of my precious, now four-year-old, daughter echoed throughout the park, I tried to remember the last time someone had called me Livvy Montgomery. Had anyone used my name recently?

Of course in an email. That had to be right. No, I was pretty sure they'd used the name Ms. Montgomery. But not Livvy. Even today while surrounded by my parents, brother, and a couple other family members, they hadn't addressed me by name.

I was now Mom. Mommy. Although Amelia calling me Mom instead of just Mommy was like a stab to the heart. I didn't like the idea that my baby girl no longer only called me Mommy.

All of that whirled in my brain in a moment's time as I turned toward Amelia and smiled.

"Hello, baby girl. What did you want to show me?" I asked, looking down at my precious daughter.

She had just gotten a haircut, and while I once again had saved a few clippings because my baby girl was growing up too quickly, she looked a mess. But she was *my* mess.

Her blonde hair was stick straight, so unlike mine it was a little disturbing. She had full bangs and pigtails on either side of her head that made me want to whip out my phone and once again take a photo. The number of albums I had labeled Amelia was a little ridiculous.

I heard the sound of a phone camera clicking come from my right, and I looked over at my mother who was indeed taking a photo.

Shea Montgomery just blinked at me with those all too innocent eyes. "What? She's cute. And she's my grandbaby. Let me be."

"I was just thinking the same. Send me that?" I asked as I moved toward Amelia.

My mother grinned and quickly texted me the photo. I looked over at Amelia, who held up her hands covered in finger paint, and sighed thinking of the mess we'd be cleaning up later.

"What did you paint today, darling?"

"Uncle John. Of course." She rolled her eyes, and I swallowed hard, wondering where she had learned that. Honestly, probably me. I was a single mother working on little sleep and I tended to roll my eyes often. Only when had my baby girl grown to the point that she could roll her eyes and look like a teenager? Yes, she was still only four, but I could blink and suddenly she'd be rolling her eyes when I wouldn't let her have the car keys for the night.

Though at Amelia's words, I looked down at my younger brother and held back a laugh. Only I couldn't stop the smile crossing my face. Once again, my mother snapped a few photos.

"Baby girl, I do believe your painting should be in the Louvre."

"What's a Loo Vee?" Amelia asked, a grin on that painted face.

I knelt down in front of her, baby wipes in hand. "It's a special museum in Paris, France."

"Where's France?"

"It is a country in Europe. Do you remember us talking about Europe?"

"Maybe. Is it with the fish and chips?"

My lips twitched. "Close."

"They have baguettes and cheese," John put in. My twenty-year-old brother sat up, his face covered in paint.

"Cheese?" Amelia asked, her eyes widening.

"Well, if there was any doubt that she was a Montgomery," my mom muttered.

I grinned up at her.

"Excuse me, you married into the family ma'am."

"I did, and I went through cheese school to understand the true depths of my love of all things dairy. Don't worry, I promise that we'll have cheesecake for dessert."

"Cake! Cake!"

I narrowed my eyes at my mother, who just fluttered her eyelashes and helped wash off Amelia.

John leaned forward, a fake pout on his face. "Hey, you're my mom. You're supposed to help wipe my face."

"You're in college, my boy. You should be able to do it yourself." And then Mom leaned forward and began to wipe off his face anyway.

He beamed over at her, and I snapped a photo. "I'm sending that to your girlfriend."

John posed again. "Go for it. She loves Mom. And it would show how great I am with kids."

"You're a menace," I said, doing my best to clean up Amelia as much as possible.

"John Montgomery. Are you thinking about kids?" my mom asked, and my brother blushed beneath the face paint.

"No. I promise. I'll wait until I'm out of college, and prepared."

"Nothing prepares you for kids," my mother said sweetly.

I swallowed hard, knowing that she hit the nail right on the head. Because I hadn't been prepared for Amelia. I hadn't even been prepared for the man I thought I had loved. The man who I thought had loved me.

But Brick was long gone, no matter how hard I tried to find him.

"Why are you sad?" Amelia asked, her voice soft. Both John and my mother gave me a look, and I pasted a bright smile on my face.

"I'm just sad that I don't have cheese right now."

It wasn't quite a lie. My mother hadn't been joking when she said cheese was a Montgomery trait. Most people went along with the joke and thought we were at least good natured when it came to it. But in reality, our family just really liked cheese. It had started with a party long ago and had now catapulted into an entire branding. When people thought of the Montgomerys, they thought of cheese. Which probably wasn't the greatest thing in the world, but I didn't mind it. It just meant no matter the family event, we were going to have something we liked to eat.

"I love cheese. Do I get to try Gouda next?"

"It's Gouda for you," John put in.

I groaned. "That wasn't even a good one."

"You mean a Gouda one?" John asked, wiggling his eyebrows.

Amelia laughed, and then threw herself at her uncle. As I watched more paint smear on his clothes, I sighed and sat back on my feet. "Well, it looks like both of our children are going to need baths tonight."

"That is up to John. I passed those duties to him long ago," my mom teased.

I stood up then and held out my hand to help her. She gave me a look but let me guide her. "I'm not elderly you know. I just ran a half-marathon."

"I don't know how you got into running. The only way that I'll ever run is either because a zombie's chasing me, Amelia needs me, or if there's a cheese plate with my name on it," I added just to make my mom laugh.

Mom shrugged. "I needed something to do after I sold the business. I mean, looking at numbers all day was fine, but I wanted something just for me. And running's it. Your father thinks I'm crazy, but he loves me."

That made me smile. "I do like swimming. I should probably get back into that."

"There's a nice program at the gym near us. Do you want me to look things up for you?"

I shook my head. "Thank you, but I'll find time."

"Really? We had to pull teeth in order to get you out here today, my child. Let me help."

I grimaced, knowing she was right even as the guilt set in. "Okay fine. I'd like that."

"You know, you should also get back into riding"

I shook my head as memories of me in my little jodhpurs and helmet came back to mind.

My mother came from money. I had known that all of my life. It was why we were well off as a family, but my mother still worked. She had built her own business down in New Orleans, where she had met my father, and then had moved up to Colorado Springs with him when my dad had wanted to be with his family again. Dad and his sister and a few friends had started up Montgomery Ink Too, a franchise of the original Montgomery Ink that my uncles and aunt had started in downtown Denver.

Now there were multiple tattoo studios around the state with our name on it, and my mother had been the one to make sure that everything business-wise was set. But before she had found her calling, and now being a half-marathoner, and making sure the businesses didn't crumble, she had been the ice princess.

At least according to my father.

I didn't know the whole story other than I had never met my grandmother. I knew she was still alive because every once in a while my mother would get a letter in the mail and look sad for a few days. And then my father would make my mother smile and things would get back to normal. In the end we didn't really need my mother's family. We had my father's family, all one hundred of them. I had far too many cousins to count, and they were each and every one part of Livvy's life.

So while we didn't need my mother's family, she still had a trust fund. And that trust fund had led to extracurriculars I had been afforded while some of my friends and family hadn't. Hence being a horse girl when I was a little kid. I had never owned my own horse, but it had been a dream.

"I have not been on a horse in so long, and I don't really think it's like riding a bike."

"You never know. Count it as research." My mom's eyes sparkled as she reached for my hand and gave it a squeeze.

"Research would be nice. Though I don't think I am editing a Western anytime soon."

"Maybe one of the heroes of those books will be a cowboy."

"Maybe. Right now I'm in the middle of editing a sci-fi though."

"No space horses?" Mom asked.

"Not yet."

"Get a hobby," my mom put in quickly.

"What?"

"Do something for yourself. Whether it's swimming or riding or baking. Do something that is not editing and reading or Amelia-related. You need that."

"I'm really busy, Mom. I have a life. I love my life."

"I know you do, but you need things for you that are Livvy, not being a mom."

The fact my mother had echoed my earlier thoughts might have worried me, but I knew she had probably gone through the same things. Didn't all mothers at one point have an identity crisis?

It didn't help that I still had nightmares one day Brick would come back and fight for custody.

I hadn't spoken to him since Amelia had been born, but he used to send letters, just to threaten me. We kept every one of them, but he always said that he would come back, and wanted to make sure his legacy was taken care of.

It was a disgusting mess, and I hadn't heard from him in nearly a year now.

And while I knew the courts had to be on my side, I wasn't certain. So I had my cousin's security company searching for Brick. If Noah couldn't find him, then nobody could.

I just wanted Brick to finally sign over parental rights, and I would be in the clear. I didn't need child support. I just wanted freedom.

As my father crested over the hill at the other end of the park, I pushed all thoughts of Brick and my worries from my mind.

Dad was tall, bearded, and tattooed, and might've looked a little scary to some people. But he was just my dad. Most of my family members were tattooed and pierced. Considering they were in the business, it just made sense. I had a few tattoos as well, and they were far more commonplace these days.

Our family sometimes felt as if we were

completely nuclear and normal. And other times, we looked like the heathens people thought we were.

"Grandpa!" Amelia called as she ran toward my dad without looking at her surroundings.

"Amelia Montgomery. What did I say about running off?" I snapped, fear in my throat.

Fear, because we were in a public park surrounded by busy roads. Yes, the Rocky Mountains were over to the west in a glorious backdrop, but there were still strangers and cars everywhere.

"Sorry, Mommy," Amelia pouted. My dad got to her then and gave me a small smile before picking up his granddaughter.

"I'm so happy you are excited to see me. But listen to your mom, okay?" My dad asked as he tickled her belly.

"I promise, Grandpa." And then she patted his beard before kissing his cheek.

"That's my girl," Shep Montgomery said with a big smile on his face.

"She's a menace," I said with a laugh as I moved forward and kissed my dad on his other cheek.

"There's both of my girls."

My dad had been the best father a girl could ask for. Seriously. When I had shown up on their doorstep fresh out of college, pregnant, and alone, they had immediately taken me in and helped me figure out what I was going to do. I had known that with my dual degrees of journalism and English literature I wanted to go into publishing but starting off as an intern and moving out to New York like they did in the movies just wasn't going to happen. Not only was it unaffordable, I was a mother now. So thanks to my mother's tutelage, I'd begun my own business. I was a freelance content editor, and also wrote articles when needed. I was a full business, with a waitlist for clients. I worked with publishers, indie authors, and hybrid ones too. It wasn't glamorous, and I wasn't rolling in Gucci bags, but it provided a living for my daughter. And I knew that I was privileged to do so because my parents had supported me.

Brick had come from more money than my mother had. And if he had paid even an ounce of child support, I wouldn't wake up in a cold sweat every once in a while, wondering what would happen if my career changed. What would be my backup for my backup.

"I'm sorry for taking so long to get here," my dad said as he set down Amelia so she could play with John some more.

"I thought you were bringing the boys?" Mom

asked, and I nearly rolled my eyes like my daughter had earlier. Because the boys could mean any one of fifty. It could be my cousins or my dad's cousins. Honestly it was a little scary how many of them there were.

"Lex and Crew said they were going to come today. They were bringing extra cold chicken."

"Did someone say chicken?" John asked as he stood up, Amelia upside down in his arms.

"If you break my child," I warned, and John just beamed.

"They're on their way. They had to park on the other side and gave me the elder parking up front." He rolled his eyes at his comment, and I pressed my lips together trying to hide my grin.

"If you laugh young lady," my dad warned, but he was still smiling.

"Well let's get the rest of the picnic set up since they're coming soon," my mom said, though it sounded more like a question.

My dad held up both hands. "I swear they are coming. With chicken."

"I love chicken," Amelia said as she rubbed her little belly.

"Same, my child. Same," Dad added with a wink.

We cleaned up the excess paint that was thank-

13

fully water-soluble. It wouldn't hurt the environment, and it would come out of everybody's clothes and hair. It was just a mess to start with. And then we started to set out the cold salads and chips and other sandwich materials.

By the time we were ready to eat, Crew and Lexington came forward, each with a bucket of chicken in hand.

"Sorry we're late. Work thing," Lex offered.

I didn't ask Lex, but I grinned up at him as he kissed the top of my head.

"Hello, cousin of mine."

"Hello there, cousin," I teased.

Technically Lex and I were second cousins or first cousins twice removed. We didn't do the math like that. Everybody in our generation were cousins and we just went with it.

It was far easier for secret Santas during holiday time.

"There's my girl," Lexington said as he held out his arms, and Amelia threw herself into them.

"One day she's going to get so tall she's going to knock me right over," Lexington teased.

"Don't age her so quickly," I said, my hand on my stomach.

"Hey there," Crew said as he took a seat next to me.

I smiled up at the man who wasn't a Montgomery but had dated a couple. In fact, most people were of the opinion that Crew and Lex were dating, though they weren't saying anything about it. I didn't ask questions, and in the end it didn't matter. I just liked Crew.

"Okay let's eat before this child starts to eat my arm," Lex said with a laugh, while Amelia chomped down on his forearm.

"Don't bite your uncle," I teased.

"Okay." Amelia rolled her eyes again and sighed and winced.

I was going to have to make that stop somehow, even though it was so cute.

Taking a day to have a picnic wasn't something I did often. Frankly, it was only Montgomery gatherings that got me out of the house. I didn't date, despite what my friends sometimes tried to make me do, and I rarely went out.

But times like this allowed me to relax just a little bit.

"Can I go throw this away?" Amelia asked, holding up the tiny trash bag.

I looked over at the trash can that was only six

15

feet away or so and frowned. "Let me come with you. Or one of your uncles."

"I'm fine. It's right there, Mommy," she whined, glaring at me.

"Watch that face of yours," I warned.

She immediately smiled. "I'm sorry. But please? I'm a big girl now."

"Fine. But I'm watching you."

It was seriously less than six feet away, and nobody was standing by the trash can. She would be fine. And I needed to stop being a helicopter parent. But she was only four. I should've still been able to wrap her in cotton wool.

The guys had gotten up to play some form of a soccer game with a few other strangers, and my mother had her back turned, finishing cleaning up some of the art supplies.

That's why they didn't see the bike coming first.

Everything happened in slow motion as I moved as quickly as I could toward my daughter.

Amelia had just put the trash in the can, smiling wide because she could reach now, as the bicyclist on his phone went off the path. Somebody screamed, another person shouted obscenities, but I only had eyes for my daughter.

When she looked up, she froze for just an instant, and I knew that bicycle was going to hit her.

Then Amelia jumped to the side, right out of the way of the bicyclist, only she was right at the edge of the curb.

A scream tore through my throat as I shifted toward her, hand outstretched, but I was too late. My little girl tripped over the side of the curb and fell right toward the busy street.

And her little scream would haunt me until my dying breath.

two

EWAN

WHILE THE WORLD moved in slow motion, I felt as though I should have seen this whole thing coming.

The gorgeous woman with blonde hair and bright blue eyes had caught my gaze from the moment I'd stepped into this park. Her smile had pulled my attention as well, even though I'd been trying to focus on my friends.

But every once in a while she would speak to her daughter, and I couldn't help but look over at her, trying to act subtle. Considering I was six foot five, broad shouldered, and hadn't bothered to change out of my boots from when I had driven down from the ranch, I already stood out. I wasn't good at being subtle.

Yet the woman had been in my peripheral vision for most of the afternoon. Even when I had tried to do my best to catch sight of the little girl's father. Only I hadn't seen a ring on that woman's finger, and my odd relief was a kick to the chest that didn't make a lick of sense.

But all of that didn't matter in the end. Because I could see what would happen next in slow motion and vivid pictures.

The little girl was trying to be so strong, a big girl as she said, throwing away her own trash. The mom wasn't that far away. Honestly, she could have taken two steps and grabbed her kid.

But when the bicyclist went off the trail, I *moved*. I didn't even realize I was moving away from my friends as somebody shouted behind me, and I took two large steps toward the little girl. At first, I hadn't wanted her to hit her head or scrape her knee, and then the horn honking from beside me filled my gut with dread.

As the little girl tripped over the curb and toward a car ready to parallel park, I gripped the back of her overalls and tugged her toward me. The shift of momentum and gravity had me falling backward myself, and I hit the ground, the little girl clutched to my chest.

I held back the curse that echoed in my mind as I tried to keep my heart rate calm. In that moment, the little girl froze in my hold. She held her breath, looking down at me with wide, slightly panicked eyes. Then everything moved back to real time.

"Amelia!"

"Oh my God, Ewan!"

Other people screamed as the driver of the car got out, her hands over her mouth. "I didn't see her. She just fell into the street. Is she okay?"

"Amelia," the blonde woman shouted.

I sat up, the kid wrapped in my arms, then the little girl was plucked from my hold, and the blonde woman held her child to her chest, rocking her back and forth.

"I'm so sorry. I'm so sorry."

"I'm okay, Mommy. I'm okay."

I found myself still sitting, arms resting on my knees as I looked up at the little girl who was patting the tears off her mother's cheeks. I didn't realize I was surrounded by others, heat crawling up my neck, until a familiar voice pulled me out of my thoughts.

"Ewan?"

I looked up into that familiar face as Crew held at his hand. "How the hell did you move so fast?"

I put my hand in his as he helped me to my feet, and I tried to ignore the group of people surrounding us. I really didn't like crowds. "She's smaller than a calf, so I've had practice."

The other man looked like he wanted to laugh, but I still saw the gray pallor beneath his skin. I didn't know how Crew knew the little girl, but he seemed to have been as scared as the mom.

"Ewan, so glad that you were there," Jackson said from my side, and I looked over at my friend who ran his hand through his beard. "I knew you were fast, but damn." My friend, and the reason I was down in Colorado Springs, winced. "Sorry ma'am."

The little girl's mom let out a shaky breath. "We curse a lot in this family. It's fine. Seriously, thank you so much," she directed at me.

I finally forced myself to look at the blonde woman with pixie-like features and blue eyes that were even more startling close up.

The girl in her arms was like a little clone of her mother. Adorable cheeks, same eyes, and straight blonde hair—though her mother's seemed to have a bit of a curl. Her pigtails had come out when I had pulled her back, so she looked a little bedraggled, but not too badly.

"I'm just glad I saw her in time. Did that cyclist

really leave?" I looked over my shoulder, scowling when I didn't see a single biker in sight.

"Yes, he just left." Her jaw tightened before it looked as if she forced herself to relax marginally. "And I'm never letting you out of my sight again." She continued to press kisses all over her daughter's face, who just giggled and looked none-worse-for-wear. If anything, all the adults looked like they had lost ten years off their life, while she seemed perfectly content.

Out of the corner of my eye, I saw another familiar face go over to the woman who had stopped parking halfway and led her into her spot. It wasn't her fault; she was following all the rules of the road, but accidents happened. She came over quickly and said she was sorry, and then ran off to her appointment in the business center across the park.

Everyone talked very quickly, and I just stood there, hands in my pockets beside Jackson.

"So Ewan, what are you doing down in Colorado Springs?" Crew asked, and I realized the man who had gone over to the driver had to be Lexington Montgomery. It had been a while since I had seen these two guys, but they hadn't changed in the past year or so since they had come up for the rodeo.

"Jackson's wedding prep," I said, pointing my

thumb at the other man. "I don't know if you guys have met."

"Can't say that I have," Jackson said as he held out his hand. "It's good to meet you two. Maybe after better circumstances. You guys are the Montgomerys right? The ones that came up to help Crew's family?"

"I'm the Montgomery. He's just the add-on." Lexington grinned as Crew rolled his eyes.

"So you three know each other?" the mother said as she stared at me, confusion in her gaze.

"A little bit. Good timing, it seems." I looked down at the little girl in her arms and tried to smile. I wasn't great with kids, as they tended to be afraid of the big beard and tall stature. But she just grinned up at me, those blue eyes wide. "You doing okay?" I asked, trying to keep the gruffness out of my voice. The whole incident had scared the shit out of me even though I hadn't let myself think too hard about that.

"Uh-huh. Mommy says to say thank you."

My lips twitched as the woman winced. "Well you're welcome."

"Thank you." She beamed at me, and I just shook my head, a smile finally playing on my face.

"She sure does look like you," I said, surprising myself.

The woman widened her eyes before she cleared her throat. "I think so most days. I'm Livvy by the way. Livvy Montgomery."

I stole a glance at Lex who just shook his head. "Cousins. One of the two hundred of us."

I held back a laugh at that—ignoring the relief she wasn't Lex's wife. "I did hear that you guys pretty much cover the whole state of Colorado. It was odd to find one of you in Wyoming for a minute."

"Oh, you're the cowboy," a younger man said as he held out his hand. "I am John Montgomery. Livvy's brother. Lex's cousin. Usually we have name tags for this sort of thing."

The older couple introduced themselves as Livvy and John's parents, the little girl's grandparents, and everyone began talking at once, continuing to thank me. The onlookers not related to the group finally dispersed and I was grateful as I didn't really like being the center of attention. I took a step back slightly, afraid that I was going to reach out and brush Livvy's hair from her face. That would be ridiculous since I didn't even know the woman. But there was just something about her that captivated me. But doing anything about that would just end in trouble. Especially with her parents staring at me.

"Did I hear you compare my daughter to a calf earlier?" Livvy asked.

I blushed once again. "Yes ma'am."

"Oh, don't start with the ma'ams," Crew said with a chuckle. "The girls get annoyed with that here."

"Maybe he's just a little more polite than you are," Livvy said a little sharply to Crew, who just smiled widely.

"Maybe, but they like me rough."

Nearly everybody scowled at him as Amelia held out her arms. "Uncle Crew?"

He winked, completely unrepentant, as he plucked Amelia from her mother's arms. "I'm going to go take this little girl for a walk, far away from the trail. It's nice to see you again, Ewan. We should catch up if you're in town for long."

"Yeah. My number's the same."

And then he headed off with John and the grandparents, leaving me standing alone with Jackson, Lexington, and Livvy.

"Seriously, I don't know how to thank you."

"You don't have to thank me. I was just in the right place at the right time. And you would've caught her."

She shuddered. "Not fast enough. It was just the worst set of circumstances. I'm never letting her do anything on her own again." She looked past me to where Crew had taken her and I knew if she could, she'd have taken her daughter back and tried to never let her go.

"I wouldn't say that," I said quietly and winced. "Not that it's my place. But I learned the more you try to hem them in, the more they want to get out and be free."

"Are you comparing my daughter to a calf again?" she asked, her lips twitching.

There it was, that sparkle in her eyes. Maybe she wasn't as scared as she had been before. I could count that as a blessing.

Lexington gave me a look, and I barely resisted the urge to shake my head. I did not live here, and I wasn't going to encroach on the Montgomerys. I couldn't help but be enraptured by the woman at my side.

"I truly owe you. If there's anything I can do, or any of the Montgomerys because I will throw them into the lot with that, let me know."

"I can do that," I said, knowing that I wouldn't. I wasn't even going to use this as a moment to get her number. I wasn't that smooth to be honest.

An awkwardness settled in and I wasn't sure what I was supposed to say. Finally she let out a breath.

"I need to go check on her because she's probably finally starting to realize that we were scared and wants her mom."

"It's nice to meet you, Livvy Montgomery."

She smiled softly, a little bit of confusion mixing with that fear, before she headed back toward the picnic area.

Lexington cleared his throat. "Anyway, thanks for playing hero and saving my niece. I don't really want to think about what would've happened if you hadn't been there."

"But I *was* there. Best not think about the worst things when you have the future to worry about."

"Somehow that's reassuring and scary all at once," the other man said.

"I do my best." I stood there awkwardly, doing my best not to look over at Livvy. That would just be too obvious, and ridiculous. I was never going to see that woman again.

I ignored the disappointment that shouldn't have been there to begin with.

"So, why are you down here again?" Lex asked.

Jackson smiled wide. "All my pre-wedding festivities."

"So you're in the wedding then?" Lexington asked.

I nodded. "Yep. His bride-to-be and all of her friends are doing a whole event." I tried to hide the annoyance in my tone, but I didn't do a very good job since Lex just snorted.

"Well, if you guys have any time before you head out, let us know. Maybe we can get you a beer or something in thanks."

I shrugged though part of me wanted to see Livvy again—an irrational thought. "I didn't do much. No need to do that. But it was good to see you again."

"Yeah, Ewan. And it's nice to meet you, Jackson." Lex finally went over to the picnic area where the others had gathered.

Jackson shook his head. "That scared the shit out of me. And I didn't even see all of it."

I'd do my best not to think of those scenarios at all, though I had a feeling I'd have a few nightmares over it. "Well, she's safe. And now we can head on to whatever is next on the list."

"I don't know why you don't sound excited about it. I'm getting married."

"And I'm somehow your best man. Didn't you have other friends?" I asked, shoving at his shoulder. We made our way to the other side of the park over the hill where Jackson's friends and family were situated. And I did my best not to look behind me. Because if I did, I would want to see if Livvy was watching me.

And I wasn't quite sure which answer I wanted to that question.

Jackson immediately moved to his fiancée, Kandi's, side, and dipped her into a kiss that had all of the women swooning.

"What took you so long?" she asked as she stood up, her cheeks blushed.

"Well this cowboy Ewan over here had to go save the day."

At their curious glances, he explained it all, making me sound far more heroic than I was.

Kandi looked over at me, wide eyes. "And she's okay? That little girl?"

"It wasn't anything. She would've been fine."

Although she had been damn close to that car, and I tried not to think about it. I had a feeling it was going to echo in my dreams for far longer than I wanted. Same with the scream that had ripped from Livvy's throat.

I couldn't imagine how scared she had been, but I didn't have to imagine anything else. Because Amelia was safe. And I wasn't going to look back at the Montgomerys. No good could come from that.

"Well, where was the mother?" Trish asked, and I did my best not to sneer or growl at the maid of honor. Trisha decided because we were walking down the aisle together, we had to do everything together. I was trying to be a good sport about it, but honestly, it hurt my brain to think about being alone in a room with her for longer than thirty seconds. Everything she said sounded like a complaint, even if she was trying to be nice about it. And I wasn't quite sure Trish knew how to be nice.

She hadn't liked the flowers Kandi had chosen, hadn't liked the setting, and was the reason we were down in Colorado Springs doing a local brew tour and celebration rather than up in Wyoming seven hours away where the wedding was going to be.

Jackson's family owned the spread next to my family's. While Jackson's was far bigger than ours, we had over five thousand acres, and it wasn't as if we were anything small. We each raised cattle, and shared water rights on some of the boundaries, and had grown up together.

Kandi and Trish as well as the other bridesmaids were born and raised in Cheyenne. And while it wasn't the huge metropolis Denver felt like, they still didn't like ranch life. I had a feeling Kandi was going to fit right in once she found her footing, but Trish hated everything to do with having the wedding on Jackson's ancestral family home.

It didn't make any sense in the grand scheme of things considering she constantly tried to get me alone and in bed. It wasn't as if I was going to move away from my ranch anytime soon.

"She was right there. It was just poor circumstances the little girl fell the wrong way."

"Well, that sounds like poor parenting. She should have been right by her little girl the whole time. Someone should do something about that."

"You're going to want to back away from that, Trish," I warned, and hadn't realized my voice had gone dangerously low until her eyes widened slightly.

Jackson cleared his throat as he wrapped his arm around Kandi's waist. "It was just an accident. But this hero here made sure the little girl was safe and is going home safely with her single mother."

My gaze shot to Jackson. "What?"

Jackson gave me a wink. "I was asking the right questions, and it seems that Ms. Livvy is currently single."

I cleared my throat. "She seems to be raising that little girl right. Even with having to do it all by herself." I hoped I sounded nonchalant, but with the way that Jackson and Kandi were both grinning at me, while Trish and the others glared, I had a feeling that I wasn't doing very good about that.

"Maybe *she* can be your date to the wedding," Trish said, her voice sickly sweet.

I froze, my shoulders tightening. Because I had forgotten I had lied to them and said I had a date. It wasn't that I couldn't get one, I just hadn't had time. And Trish had been angling for that position.

Jackson gave me a look, and I just swallowed hard, trying to look like I wasn't lying. "Don't worry about me. I'll be there with bells on, and you don't have to worry about my date. She'll be there too."

A complete lie, but that just meant I was going to have to fix that soon. Because Trish and Kandi and the others weren't going to take no for an answer. Meaning I would have to find a date within the week to drive up with me to Wyoming for a wedding. Totally easy. Not insurmountable.

And it would be better off for everyone if I pushed the thought of Livvy and that beautiful smile of hers out of my mind.

Because I was never going to see Livvy Montgomery again.

three

LIVVY

AMELIA RAN across the park with Aria on her heels. I held back my wince and my mothering urge to call out to them and tell them to be careful. I didn't think I was going to be able to calm down and act rationally when it came to my daughter anytime soon. That first night after the near accident, I'd ended up sleeping on the floor in her room, aware I was on the verge of hovering too much. But I'd woken up every hour to watch the rise and fall of her chest—just to make sure I hadn't been dreaming of the worst.

I could still see her little scared face as she fell back into the road.

I don't know what I would've done if Ewan hadn't been there to catch her.

No, I wasn't going to think about that again.

I also tried not to think about Ewan at all. Considering the night after, it had taken all my strength to not dream about him. I had woken up in a sweat more than once. Of course, most of it had been because of Amelia. I had kept imagining what could've happened if the cyclist hadn't been there, if I had been closer.

Or if Ewan had not.

I held back a shudder. I was not going to continue to think of worst-case scenarios. The more I did, the more I knew I would not be able to sleep anytime soon.

Only, it wasn't that worst-case scenario that had kept me up the past two nights.

No, it was also about that damn sexy cowboy. I wasn't in the mood for the space to think about a man like that.

My friends and family had been trying to get me out of the house more often lately. Everybody was so kind when it came to me being a single mother. However, I felt as if they wanted me to continue to reach out and want more. But I didn't want any more. I liked where I was.

I loved my daughter. I loved my job. And I didn't want to ruin anything by wanting more.

As it was, I couldn't think about the future when the past still had its claws deep inside, trying to dig its way through my soul and promises.

Because I could not find Brick.

I had been so young and stupid when I thought I had fallen for him. I had thought he could give me the world and he had done a good job faking it.

He had been so kind, so caring. He also had been good in bed, and always made sure I was taken care of when we were out.

But one positive pregnancy test later, and he had run away. He hadn't even bothered to run with his tail between his legs. No, he had run with his chin held high and two middle fingers in the air.

And I hated him more with each passing day. I knew it wasn't healthy. I knew I shouldn't think about him at all. He had never met his daughter—had never even cared to reach out.

It was his loss. I knew that.

Yet there was always some part of me that was afraid he would show up and try to take my daughter from me. It didn't make any sense, but his family had connections. If they *bothered*, they could. They had that power.

And their power scared me more than anything.

Only, we couldn't find him to ensure my daughter was safe in my arms for eternity.

Part of me hoped he had run away and never wanted to look back. His family didn't contact us, and while I appreciated that, I could not sever that connection fully without knowing where he was. And honestly, it worried me that Montgomery Security—my family's company who could find *anyone* and keep them safe—couldn't find Brick.

Because what was my ex hiding?

And when would he come back so my own choices would haunt me as they always did.

It didn't help that Amelia was starting to ask more questions about her daddy. She had been so enamored with all of the men in my family, that I had hoped that would be enough. That I would be enough.

Between my father, brother, cousins, and uncles, I had hoped there would be enough men in her life that she would not feel the lack of not having a father around.

But now she wanted to know him.

And I didn't have any answers for her.

She was far too young, far too precious. And I was failing as a mother. I knew that.

Only I was out of options on how to make things better.

"Earth to Livvy," Aria said from my side.

I jolted out of my thoughts and turned to my cousin. Before I could say anything, however, Amelia jumped into my arms and I fell back on the blanket, all three of us laughing until our sides hurt. I set my daughter up with her snack and bubble water and tried to be content with what we had, rather than worry for what *could* have happened.

I looked over at Aria and forced a smile, pushing those thoughts from my head. She had her dark hair pulled back from her face in a twisted knot that had mostly come undone. And somehow it totally worked for her.

My cousin also had that odd look in her eyes that told me she was just as far deep into her thoughts as I was.

I wanted to help Aria. We all did. But she was never going to allow us.

And Aria wasn't one to ask for help.

The call is coming from inside the house.

Because yes, I was just the same. It worried me that both of us pushed away thoughts of help and our families when we needed them the most. Considering how amazing our families were. Perhaps that was the problem. Everybody was so good at what they did, so selfless, that it was hard to be the one who needed help.

"Sorry. I'm delighted that you're out here today."

Aria studied my face for a moment, and a small smile appeared. "I'm glad I'm here too. I've been lost in the woods recently with my latest project. So it's good for me to get out a bit more."

"Can you talk about your project?" I asked, as interested in her art as ever.

"Soon. I'm just trying to get in the thick of it. You know me. Once I start talking about it too much, I either lose interest, or I screw up."

"No that's not the case." I scratched my nose. "I loved your latest venture. The show was absolutely stunning."

A blush crossed Aria's cheeks, and she did that shrug she always did when she didn't like taking compliments. I didn't blame her since I was the same. "It helps our family owns the gallery."

I rolled my eyes. "The family doesn't show random art pieces that are better placed on the fridge. And it's not just family who gets in."

"True. Although I would love it if Nate would let us show one of his pieces."

I smiled, thinking of our cousin Nate. He was

Uncle Storm and Everly's son, and a brilliant painter. But he didn't want us showing off his work. In fact, most of the artists in our family tended to try to keep their work away from the Montgomery gallery.

While I didn't work in that field or in the building the Montgomerys owned, many of my cousins did.

On one side of the building was Montgomery Security, where Aria had worked for a short time. They were private security, bodyguards, and also installed security systems for those who needed it. Next to that was Montgomery Legacy, the tattoo shop that another set of cousins owned and operated. It wasn't the first of its ilk in our family, considering my father owned another branch, but each person in my family who worked with art had a different medium. A different specialty. Next to that was Latte on the Rocks, a coffee shop and bakery that hadn't technically been owned by the Montgomerys at first, but of course, the women who owned it married into the family. Apparently, that's what we did. If we didn't own something, we married the owners.

The business next door had once been a bike shop, though our family didn't like to think about that. The operator had hidden a dark side that none of us had seen until it had almost been too late. But now it was family only under our roof. And while that section was a gallery for certain nights, it was also a school for those who wanted to learn different mediums.

Everybody was so talented, and I wish I could do something other than draw stick figures with slightly disproportionate limbs.

"Mommy? Can I have ice cream?"

I looked down at the grapes in her hand before leaning over to tap her nose with my finger. "I thought you already had your snack, Amelia Montgomery."

My daughter looked up at me with those bright blue eyes and fluttered her eyelashes. I barely resisted the urge to narrow my gaze because I was pretty sure the woman at my left had taught her that trick.

"But I ate my fruit. I've been really good."

"She has you there."

I scowled at my best friend and cousin, wondering what I had done to deserve all of this cuteness. "Well, I'm glad that I had already planned on making sure we were near your favorite place with soft serve."

Amelia stood up, her hands in the air. "Yay!"

I swallowed hard, tears threatening as I looked at my baby girl. She was so happy. I knew that we would grow together, and she would hit her teenage years, and things would be different. For now though, I'd treasure these moments.

And if my baby wanted ice cream, she was going to get ice cream. Because she never asked for much.

"Okay, my darling terror, it's my turn to spoil you." Aria stood up and held out her hand, and my daughter slid hers into her aunt's.

"Be careful crossing the street," I blurted, and Aria didn't narrow her gaze at me or even roll her eyes. She just simply squeezed my daughter's hand a little tighter, and I knew she was thinking the same thing I had.

We had almost lost Amelia because of the strange set of circumstances and letting her out of our sight or reach wasn't going to happen anytime soon.

"We'll be back soon." Then Amelia's eyes widened, and her teeth bit into her lip. I did not trust that expression.

I stiffened, the hairs on the back of my neck rising. "What?"

"Oh, just a certain cowboy is behind you."

I turned quickly, nearly knocking myself over onto the blankets, and there he was.

Ewan.

I nearly questioned how Aria would even know what this man looked like, and then I remembered that Lex had shown his photo to everyone so they could have an idea of what he looked like as he told the story.

It had taken everything within me not to ask for that photo myself. There was something wrong with me.

We weren't in the same park as before, but we were close to it. In fact we were near a common event center where I knew they had planned activities for weddings. I wasn't quite sure what exactly they did, but it was commonplace to see groups of people preparing for their nuptials.

So it would make sense if Ewan had been close by already, that he might be here.

In all the parks in all the world.

His back was to me though, and he didn't see me, and I was grateful for that. He probably didn't need to see the drool currently sliding down my chin.

"Ewan! Mr. Ewan!"

I cursed as the man in question turned at the sound of my daughter's voice. I noticed his eyes widen marginally before that gorgeous smile played over his face.

My heart stopped. In that moment it felt as if someone had ripped my heart ever so slightly so I could pause this time.

It didn't make any sense.

I didn't even *know* this man. It must just be a delayed reaction for him saving my daughter's life.

And not because I found him attractive or anything.

"Whoa," Aria said, and I glared at her.

Amelia waved and Ewan did the same while I tried to ignore my ovaries screaming in glee.

"I'm going to pack up and put everything in the car. Why don't you go get her ice cream now."

"Sure. But don't you think it's a coincidence that he and his group are here?" she asked, her voice far too casual.

And as I narrowed my gaze at her, I realized that her plan for this park hadn't been a coincidence at all. Yes, I had wanted one near an ice cream shop my daughter would like, but it had been Aria's idea for this exact one. Oh, she had *known* he might be here.

Either she wanted to get a good look at him, or perhaps my cousin had seen far too much.

Well crap.

"Why don't you head over to that ice cream shop? We can discuss this later."

My cousin beamed as she and Amelia skipped off to get ice cream, and I packed up our small basket of things.

Ewan had gone back to his conversation after smiling over at us and I knew that was a good thing. It wasn't as if I truly knew this man. He was just an acquaintance of my family. One who had been there at the right time. Nothing more. Nothing less.

I was not going to think about a certain dream I'd had of him before.

A blush stained my cheeks as I made my way to my car and stuffed everything into the back.

"Does he really have a date to the wedding? Or is he just saying this to save face?" a woman asked from two cars down. I couldn't see who she was, and I knew she couldn't see me, but for some reason her voice carried.

"He's lying. Ewan is just playing hard to get. Don't you worry, I'll make sure he's not single for long."

"Trish, you're terrible. Ewan is a nice guy," another woman said.

However, I had frozen at the sound of Ewan's name. Were these women going to the same wedding? And Ewan had date. Or at least they were questioning if he did. I didn't know why that was any of my business, or why my body was reacting in any sort of way. But I swallowed hard and gently closed the door so I didn't startle them and they wouldn't know I had been eavesdropping.

"When Kandi started dating Jackson, she promised she would try to set me up with him. And it hasn't happened yet. I'm tired of dating small town boys. I want a real man, with a real job, and a real future."

"You mean a big bank account with the vast spread of acreage," a third woman said slyly.

"I can't help it if I like pretty things. And Ewan could get me pretty things."

My hands twisted on my purse strap, and part of me wanted to go over and ask what the hell that woman was thinking. But again, it was none of my business.

Of course, I thought I should probably tell Ewan people were talking about him like he was a large bank account with a blank checkbook. Right? I could mention it to Lexington, and he could mention it to Ewan. That way I wouldn't have to speak to the man who made me all fluttery inside.

Then again it wasn't any of my business. And from what I could tell, Ewan didn't have any trouble brushing this woman off. Apparently he'd declined to being her date.

Because he already had one.

Again I ignored the little twinge and quietly made my way out of the parking lot so I could meet up with Aria.

I turned the corner and ran smack into a rock-hard chest. My hands went right to that chest, and I froze, realizing exactly who I'd run into.

Ewan had put his hands on my hips to steady me, and neither one of us moved as we were pressed firmly against one another, my breath oddly quickening.

I had met my share of pretty men, handsome men, rugged ones. But for some reason that strong jaw line of his did something to me. I needed to be aware of that though. I had fallen for a pretty face before. And while I had gotten the love of my life out of it with Amelia, I had lost something as well.

Just like that, I cooled slightly.

"I thought that was you across the park," his deep voice said, and once again I was all warm deep inside.

How could he make me hot so quickly?

"I thought that was you as well," I said lamely. "Thank you for waving."

I could have hit myself.

"Where's Amelia?" he asked as he looked over my head, and part of me softened inside. Because of course he would ask after the little girl that he saved. Damn it. That man needed to stop being desirable. Or at least not be so interesting.

"She should be back on her way with ice cream with her aunt." I cleared my throat and realized we were both still touching each other. Ewan didn't immediately let go. Instead he squeezed my hips ever so slightly before taking a step back. I ran my hands down my thighs, feeling awkwardly bereft at the lack of contact. I had clearly been losing my mind and needed to get laid. It had been far too long.

"I should probably tell you something," I blurted, wondering why I was getting in the middle of it.

His brow rose. "Okay. Actually I'm glad I caught you because I was here to ask you something. But what is it?" Worry etched on his face.

My teeth bit into my lip before I finally allowed myself to get in the middle of whatever *this* was. "I don't know if it's you, but somebody mentioned your name." I was whispering before I looked over my shoulder to see if the women had come this way. Thankfully it looked like they had gone to the other side of the parking lot.

Ewan followed my gaze, and I watched as his jaw tightened ever so slightly.

"Let me guess, the bridal party said something to you?" He stared me down, and I swallowed hard. "Did they hurt you?"

My eyes widened. "No. I don't know them, and they didn't even say a word to me. But I think they were talking about you." I swallowed hard once again and told him what they said.

Ewan groaned and pinched the bridge of his nose. "Hell. I do not know why that woman won't take no for an answer."

"I kind of explained why she won't," I said gently.

Ewan snorted. "Yes, the size of my…ranch."

I burst out laughing, and he chuckled right along with me. A deep chuckle that vibrated inside me.

"I would just be careful at the wedding since she doesn't think you have a date or wants to replace them." That sobered me slightly at the reminder. "And I would warn your date."

Ewan winced and put his hands in his pockets. "About that…" His voice trailed off, and I licked my lips. His gaze went straight to my mouth at the action, and I froze.

"About what?" I asked, my voice oddly breathy.

"You said you owe me."

I blinked, not sure where he was going with this. "Of course I do. You saved Amelia. I'll do anything." I pause. "Within reason."

His lips twitched at that. "I lied to Trish and the others. I don't have a date." My heart did that twist thing once more, and I did my best to ignore it. "Will you pretend to be my date?" He paused. "And pretend that I asked you long before this."

I blinked, utterly surprised. "You want me to be your fake date to your best friend's wedding?"

He ran his hand over the back of his neck, a blush creeping up his face. It was oddly sexy.

"Okay, maybe we can't pretend that I asked you long before this since they know I met you when I caught Amelia."

"That makes sense. You can't really reinvent history," I said, trying to figure out exactly what he wanted. And exactly what I was going to say.

"No, I can't. And I would ask you to be my real date to the wedding, but I have a feeling you would say no."

He met my gaze, and I had to wonder exactly how he had known that. Because I didn't know him. Yet, if he'd asked me out on a true date, to a wedding or anywhere else, I would have said no.

Because there was something about him that made me want to scream yes.

The last time I had said yes in that fashion, I had gained the most precious point of my life but lost everything else in the process. I didn't trust myself. I didn't trust my own desires.

Therefore I didn't date.

Only he was trying to get me out of my comfort space...and I indeed owed him. Yet how did he know what I would say without even asking?

That worried me, and yet, I wanted an excuse.

My failing once again.

"What exactly are you asking, Ewan?" I asked softly.

"Be my fake date to the wedding. Protect me from Trish and the others." His lips quirked into a smile. "Don't make me a complete liar to my friends."

"You're serious."

"I'll come up with an excuse, a timeline of how things worked out, but come with me. Just as friends." He cleared his throat, and I bit my lip. "No pressure. No worries. Just really good food, and you have to deal with me in a tux."

I nearly had to clamp my thighs together at the

image. Because…wow. "This doesn't make any sense."

"It doesn't have to. But please save me from the wedding party. Help me, Livvy. You're my only hope."

I laughed out loud at that, knowing I was crazy to even think about saying yes.

Only I didn't want to say no. I wanted to take the leap and not look down. Damn the consequences.

"Okay. I can be your fake date."

At my response, his smile brightened, and I saw Aria and Amelia out of the corner of my eye coming toward us.

I really hoped I knew what I was doing.

four
EWAN

"WHEN I'D SAID yes to being your date, even your fake date, I probably should have asked *where* this wedding was being held," Livvy said dryly. She looked past me and over the vast lands of Wyoming, and I inhaled a deep breath over the place I'd always called home.

Clover Lake was a small town in northern Wyoming complete with creeks, large swaths of land, nosy neighbors, that small town feel, and of course, the large lake that gave the town its name. My family had been part of it for generations and we knew nearly every soul that resided in our town. We also employed quite a large number of them. My brothers, sister, and I had rode wild over the town and Clover Lake had stories to tell.

But today wasn't about that.

Though I held back a wince at her words, mostly because I wasn't sure what I was supposed to say. It wasn't that I'd intentionally mislead Livvy. But I'd also needed her to say yes. I didn't know what was wrong with me other than I'd *needed* her by my side.

Since that feeling had never run through me before in my life, it was a little difficult to get used to.

Yet as we walked through Jackson's family ranch, I couldn't help but be relieved and...oddly excited she was here. And excited wasn't usually a word used to describe me. At all.

Of all my family, I was the quiet one. Not that I wanted to hide, more like I didn't have much to say in a family that had everything to say. With four brothers and a baby sister, my family nearly rivaled Livvy's. Although I wasn't sure anyone could rival the Montgomerys.

"I thought I'd mentioned it," I finally answered, realizing that I'd been quiet for far too long. I was already awkward as hell with this far-fetched idea of bringing a practical stranger to my best friend's wedding. But perhaps I did need the protection of a date to Jackson's nuptials. And wasn't that a hard pill to swallow.

"No, you hadn't," Livvy said with a laugh. "Though I supposed I should have guessed since neither of you are from Colorado. I was just confused since so many of the pre-wedding activities took place in Denver or Colorado Springs." She paused. "And there sure seemed to be a lot of them." I held back a grin at the laughter in her gaze.

There was just something about Livvy Montgomery that made me lose my thoughts and just want to look into those deep blue eyes of hers. The only other two times I'd seen her, she'd either been scared out of her mind or apprehensive. And yet both times I'd wanted more.

And now there was a chance for more. All because she'd come with me to Wyoming for a wedding, leaving her daughter with her parents.

If that wasn't a crazy thing to do, I wasn't sure what was. Perhaps both of us hadn't been thinking clearly. But she was with me and there was no going back at this point. The whole thing was a completely ridiculous scenario I was sure wasn't going to work, and yet I still didn't mind. The excuse had been worth it.

"I didn't realize how many events are part of a wedding. Hell, this is the first wedding I've ever been in. Maybe it's the norm."

Livvy's eyes danced. "I don't think it's the norm. Then again, I've never been a bridesmaid."

My eyebrows lifted. "I find that hard to believe. How many friends and cousins do you have?"

"Not all of them are married yet, and most of my family have gone small when it came to their nuptials. Meaning only one or two people standing up for them."

"There's no hope you'll be able to help us figure out what we're supposed to be doing."

"Completely hopeless."

We were leaning against each other, and I wasn't even sure either one of us had noticed until that moment. I took a step back, clearing my throat. It wouldn't be good to make a move on her when she was just doing me a favor.

Finaly, her shoulders relaxed, and she spoke. "You said this is your first time in a wedding. So your siblings aren't married yet?"

"No," I said with a shake of my head. "All four of my older brothers and my younger sister aren't anywhere close to that." Much to my parents' chagrin.

"You are just like some sets of my cousins. So many siblings. I don't know how your parents did it."

"Frankly, neither do I. Not to mention Jackson

was an only child, and he was over at my place more often than not. So it was like another brother."

Livvy's smile softened. "That's nice. He had you."

I shrugged. "We've always had each other's backs. Hence why I said yes to this wedding and everything that came with it. Jackson and Kandi love each other and get along to the point they just fit. So I don't mind." Even when I was bored or uncomfortable. Then again, the events allowed me to meet Livvy. So maybe it wasn't all bad.

"The way they seem to be with each other makes me think that this whole marriage thing will be worth it to them."

There was something in her tone, it made me once again want to ask about Amelia's father. I didn't, but it was damn hard to hold back the question.

"Ewan," a soft voice said from behind me, and I stiffened. Livvy slid her hand into mine, mingling our fingers together. She gave my hand a squeeze and met my gaze. And just like that, my shoulders relaxed marginally, and I turned with Livvy on my arm.

"Trish. You ready for the wedding?"

"Tonight's the rehearsal dinner. That's what

getting ready for the wedding means." Her eyes narrowed on Livvy. "This is your date? *Her?*"

I stared, wondering where the hell her attitude came from. She wasn't usually like this, albeit she had wanted more from me. Hell, none of the bridesmaids were usually like this. I liked Kandi. She was great for Jackson, and the two were thick as thieves. She truly loved him, and everyone could tell. I had thought her friends were of the same ilk. But with the way that Trish, Holland, Sarah, and Kendra were acting, maybe I was wrong.

"Her name is Livvy. And yes, she's my date. I got a plus one after all. Perks of being the best man." I gave Trish a pointed look, staring down at her. "Is there something I can help you with?"

"I thought you said you had a date before meeting her. So what, you dumped the other one because you found something better? That doesn't seem very nice."

I shook my head, wondering what was going on in that hateful mind of hers. I hadn't needed a date. I could've gone to this whole damn thing alone without having to deal with anybody's judgment. I did not care. But for some reason, the moment I had seen Livvy, something had clicked. I wanted her here. I used a damn stupid excuse, but now she was by my side. And even though I saw and felt the hesitation, I knew she liked being here too. I didn't mind calling this a fake date, but I really didn't want to be playing pretend.

"Trish, why are you so intent on figuring out my dating life? Don't you have a thousand things to do as the maid of honor? And lose the attitude. I'm done."

"I just don't think Jackson's friend should be lying."

"And maybe Kandi's friends should mind their own business," Livvy put in.

I held back a grunt, my hands fisting at my sides.

"This doesn't concern you," Trish snapped.

"Considering you're talking about me as if I'm not here, it does. And I'm not sure what your problem is, but it's not me. And it's clearly not Ewan. So while you do one of the thousand things I am sure you *should* be doing, why don't you stop worrying about things out of your control."

Trish raised her chin. "I know you're just with him for his money. But don't worry, the McBrides are never going to settle down. And if they do, it's going to be with someone from *home*. Not some city girl who uses her daughter to lure men. I bet you did the same thing to her daddy."

I moved forward then, putting myself between Livvy and Trish so that Livvy didn't end up in jail for murdering a woman.

"You are going to want to take a step back. And never, *ever* talk about that little girl again. You do? And you'll have to do deal with me. I don't know what kind of trip you're on, but it has nothing to do with me, Livvy, or the McBrides. I didn't want to date you. My brothers don't want to date you. We tried to be nice about it. Subtle even. But if you're going to continually insult my friends, and their *fucking children*, we're going to have a problem."

Trish took a step back, her eyes wide. "How could you speak to me like that?"

"You're lucky that he stepped in front of me, or that pretty face of yours wouldn't be so pretty when I was done with it," Livvy growled.

Was it weird that I got hard just hearing her speak like that? There was just something so fierce about her that nearly sent me over the edge, and I told myself I needed to stay focused.

"Are you going to let her insult me like that?"

"The only reason I'm not letting her at you is I don't want to have to deal with the sheriff. Remember, Trish. All this land that you want? It means there's also a lot of places to hide the body."

"How dare you threaten me."

"How dare you insult me and my child so maybe you can get a crumb of the money you think that Ewan has," Livvy said so calmly that I was truly afraid she was going to go through me to kill this woman.

I held up my hand as Trish went to speak and shook my head. "Go. Go now or I'm going to go talk to Kandi, and we'll see exactly how much of your lying and nastiness is about to catch up to you."

Her face paled and she scrambled back. "You're going to come crawling back."

"I was never there in the first place."

She hopped away, and I was grateful we hadn't had an audience. When I turned to look at Livvy, I knew I'd need to atone for Trish's bullshit. The woman in front of me hadn't deserved any of her ire, and it was my fault she'd been forced to.

"I'm so damn sorry. I should not have brought you up here."

Livvy just looked at me before she burst out laughing.

"What?" I asked, utterly confused. "Why are you laughing?"

"It's like she's in high school. Or at least high

school in movies from the eighties. Trish tried to emulate a cheerleader without any personality. What did she think she was going to do, use her wiles to get you into bed and force you to marry her when you're caught? What year does she think it is?"

I pressed my lips together. "Those so-called wiles would have never worked. And no matter how many shotguns her daddy has, there wouldn't be a wedding."

"Thank God. I thought you were smart. I would've hated to be wrong about that."

I reached forward and pushed her hair back behind her ear. "I'm sorry, you know. For what she said about your daughter. Her father. She has no right to any of that information, and no right to degrade you like that."

Livvy reached up and gripped my hand, leaning into my palm as I cupped her cheek. "It's funny how some people look at single moms so differently than they do single dads."

I frowned as she lowered my hand but didn't let go.

"My cousin was a single father for the first five years of Nora's life, when his girlfriend died in childbirth."

"Fuck. I'm sorry."

"So am I. She was an amazing girl and we miss her to this day. And maybe it's the circumstances, but in the end, it was people looking at a single father and not judging. They were there to help, to hit on him, to do everything that they could to prove that my cousin being a dad like any good dad was some monumental feat. And yet when people figure out that Amelia doesn't have a father, I'm immediately labeled a whore."

Rage slammed into me. "You're not, and if they call you that in front of me, I'm going to be the one in jail."

Her lips twitched. "My family would say the same. I thought I was in love, and I wasn't. I was just out of college, thinking I had a steady and beautiful relationship. And the moment that pregnancy test came up positive, everything changed. Brick was no longer the caring boyfriend who talked about the future and all his dreams with his family's estate. Never my dreams, mind you. That should have been the first of many clues. When we found out I was pregnant, he was suddenly the man who called me that whore, claimed the baby couldn't be his, and left. He cut ties with his family on the surface, cut ties with me in every way possible, and never looked back. I still don't know where he is. Amelia has never met him, and I hope to hell never will. But sometimes I wake up in the middle of the night in a cold sweat because I think he will come back. And he will use his family money to try to take my daughter from me."

"Livvy. What a fucking asshole." I paused, shaking my head. "I'm trying to think of something more eloquent here, than I really want to find that man and kill him. Which probably isn't the greatest thing to say."

"You wouldn't be the only one. And yes, he is an asshole. And throughout the entire pregnancy, and the four years I've had my daughter, people judge me. They realize that my last name never changed, so therefore I couldn't have been married. Not that I would've had to change my name, but social norms in their eyes decree I should have. They ask about her father, or pointedly ignore the idea while whispering behind my back. And they judge me. I'm just another single mom out there who couldn't keep a man. While my cousin was a brave soldier who found his way into being a gentle father. The hypocrisy is ridiculous. And yet, I never blamed

Sebastian. He went through hell and has raised a beautiful little girl. And my little girl is amazing. I would walk through hell for her. And sometimes I feel like I have. So no, Trish's words didn't really bother me. Other than her talking about my daughter at all. She can lob any accusation or threat my way and I do not care. Because I have lived through it. And I'm not using my daughter's near death experience to get a man."

I reached forward and pinched her chin, bringing her toward me. Her eyes widened suddenly, and I narrowed my gaze. "I wanted you here. I'm the one who asked you to be here. If there was a way I could go back and kick Brick's ass—" I paused. "What the hell kind of name is Brick?"

Her lips widened into a smile. "Again, I don't know what I was thinking."

"But back on topic. I used the excuse of wanting to keep Trish and the others at bay to get you here. The moment I saw you at that park I wanted to get to know you. And it's ridiculous that something clicked inside me. I want to know everything about you, and I wanted more time to do so. And I want to protect you from all those people who would dare shame or judge you. And it scares me I feel it so hard already. And I'm just now getting to know you."

Livvy swallowed hard and stared up at me. "It worries me that I want the same"

And I leaned down, doing what I probably shouldn't, and brushed my lips against hers. She groaned slightly, and I parted her lips with my tongue, deepening the kiss ever so slightly.

I pulled back before anything else could happen, before it was too much, and let out a deep breath.

"There's nothing fake about that."

"No, there really wasn't." She swallowed hard again.

"Thank you for trusting me with that story. And I'm a selfish dick who wants to know more. To know everything. I want to get to know you."

"This is a completely ridiculous situation, but I'm really glad I said yes." She paused and looked up at me. "I don't date, Ewan."

My heart stopped at that, and I stared at her. "Ever?"

"Ever. At first it was because I was heartbroken. And then I had no time to date. Frankly I still don't. Between my job, Amelia, and helping out my family, it's hard for me to carve out time. I did so for this, and I am surprised at myself every single time I think about it. But I don't date because I'm so afraid that one day it's going to be Brick again. I'm going to realize I'm terrible at this."

"One bad decision, one terrible man, doesn't make you bad at this."

"Tell that to my mind at two a.m. when I can't sleep."

I slid my fingers over her shoulder, tilting my head. "So you're saying you want me to be there at two a.m. when you can't sleep?"

Livvy pressed her lips together and shook her head. "I don't know if that was a good line, or ridiculous one."

"I did ask you to be to be my fake date to a wedding. We are already past the ridiculous."

"Ewan!"

I dropped my hand but didn't move away from Livvy as I looked over my shoulder at Jackson's shout. "Hey. What's up?" I asked, hoping that neither one of them could notice my raging hard on pressing against my jeans.

"Trish is acting weird, and I wanted to make sure everything is okay." Jackson slowed down, his smile widening when he caught sight of Livvy. "Hey, I'm glad you're here. Did you bring Amelia?" he asked, looking around as if a little girl was hiding behind the bushes.

"No, she's with her grandparents. Although Ewan did invite her," she teased.

I shrugged. "I know I only got a plus one, though I figured the kid would get a kick out of all of these flowers and the horses."

"Exactly. We loved horses when we were kids."

"So did I," Livvy put in, surprisingly. "I used to ride when I was younger, and in fact my mom and I were just talking about me starting up again."

Jackson's eyes widened. "Well, you should know that Ewan is one of the best teachers out there. Our ranch handles more horses than his does since we breed them, and they mostly focus on cattle, but he's great with horses."

Livvy looked up at me then, curiosity in her gaze. "Really?"

I could stare at those eyes forever. And that meant I needed to calm the fuck down. "Really. Maybe if we have time, I'll take you for a ride."

She raised a single brow, and I rolled my eyes as Jackson burst out laughing.

"Used to be smoother than that, brother," Jackson said with a laugh.

"Shut up. Both of you. And the kid isn't here because she has a birthday party to go to the day that Livvy leaves." A day I oddly did not want to focus on.

"And frankly, it would've been a little confusing to bring her here, on top of the reason why I'm Ewan's date," Livvy added before she paused. "Considering they're already asking."

Jackson shrugged. "I'm glad you're here. I'm just sad that Lexington and Crew couldn't make it."

"I don't know if you want that many Montgomerys and honorary Montgomerys here," Livvy said dryly, and I realized I was still holding her hand, my thumb sliding along the top of it. Her skin was so soft. And Jackson hadn't missed the gesture.

"Anyway, I'm sorry Trish was acting up. I don't know what's going on with her. Hell, I don't know what's going on with any of the wedding party. Other than the love of my life I'm about to get married to, *you* are the only sane one here," Jackson said, and I saw the worry in his gaze.

"What's wrong?"

"I have no idea. People are just acting weird and out of sorts. I thought Kandi and I were supposed to be the ones stressed out. Instead, every time I see her we are both relaxed and ready to start the next phase of our life. Thank you for being the sane ones along with us," Jackson said pointedly.

I didn't like the sound of that and knew we'd

have to take care of it. Kandi and Jackson deserved the world and I'd find a way to give it to them.

Jackson winced. "Anyway, your room should be ready now, and I texted you the code to get in. We'll see you at the dinner?" he asked, and without waiting for us to answer, he jumped off to do something else. That's when Livvy stiffened at my side.

I cursed under my breath. I had picked up Livvy from the airport and we had come immediately to the ranch. The rehearsal dinner was tonight, the wedding tomorrow, and then she would fly out early the next morning. Meaning we had two nights at the immense guest house of the ranch. And since it was such a large structure, it acted as more of an inn and bed-and-breakfast.

And that meant there weren't that many rooms up for grabs.

"I completely forgot that it's only one room." I paused. "And one bed because I'm way too big for a double or queen."

I knew I was going to have to sleep on the couch tonight. Because if I was in bed with her? I wouldn't be able to keep my hands off her. Hell, I still couldn't keep my hands off her.

"I guess I didn't think that far head," Livvy said

with a shake of her head. "We will figure it out. We are adults."

I nodded tightly, realizing that it was once again probably a lie.

"Let's go get your things out of the truck, and then I'll show you the room. Pretty sure there's a couch in there."

"Okay, I'll be comfortable on the couch."

I snorted. "I'm not about to put you on the couch."

"You just said that you were too big for a queen bed." Her gaze raked over me, and she was damn lucky I had a slight restraint on my control.

"I'll be fine."

Except by the time we made it into the room, I realized there would be no figuring it out. Because there really was only room for one giant king bed. And no couch with barely any floor.

"Well hell," I said roughly as the door snapped closed behind us.

"We can make this work. It's not like we're going to be here that often anyway. We have to head right back out to the rehearsal. And that will run late. So don't worry. We'll make sure we stay on our sides of the bed." I looked at her then, and she blushed. "I'm really speaking quite quickly, aren't I?"

"If I'm in bed with you, Livvy Montgomery, I'm not going to be able to keep my hands off you."

I watched as her throat worked hard as she swallowed. "Who said I really wanted your hands off me?" she breathed, and then my hands were definitely on her.

I pinned her to the door, using one hand to lock her arms above her, as my other went straight to her thigh. She had on a tiny little dress that looked sweet and demure, but all I had been thinking about since I had seen her was rocking it up her hips just to see what she wore underneath.

"I don't have that much restraint, Montgomery."

"We both know I came here not to be your fake date."

And then my mouth was on hers, and my hand was sliding up and around to grip her ass. She arched against me, and I molded her flesh beneath me. She tasted sweet, and it was all I could do not to slide those panties to the side, shove my pants down, and slide in deep.

"Are you wet for me, Livvy? If I touch you right now, would you be wet?"

"Why is it that your voice does that to me?"

"Let's check," I whispered, my voice barely above

a growl. And I moved my hand forward, sliding her panties to the side.

"You are fucking soaked. You saying that my voice did this to you? That pretty pussy of yours is wet and ready for me?"

"I didn't realize that a cowboy talking dirty to me would nearly send me over the edge."

My lips crawled into a smile against her neck.

"You're going to end up with beard burn all over your skin. The world will know it's from me. Will you be okay with my claim on this delicate skin of yours?" I asked, my fingers sliding between her folds. She drenched my palm, her hips rocking against me.

"Please, Ewan."

"Please what?"

"Mark me. I don't care. Just stop teasing me."

I bit gently down on her flesh then, she moaned into me. Then I slid my thumb over her clit she let out a gasp.

"That's it. You're so responsive. Do you think you can come on my hand, Montgomery?"

"I don't know. Can we try?"

"Livvy." I crushed my mouth to hers as I slid two fingers deep. She let out a shocked gasp as I slid the third finger in, rotating back and forth.

"Do you hear that sound? You're so wet every

time I slide deep inside you, we can hear it. Imagine that's my cock. But I'm bigger than this, so I would stretch you. You okay with that, Livvy? With my cock stretching that tight cunt of yours?"

As I pressed against her clit again, she broke, her knees going weak as she came against me. Warm and hot against my flesh, I kissed her again, keeping her hands pinned above her head.

I had never seen such a beautiful sight as Livvy Montgomery losing control in my arms.

My dick was hard as steel, and I nearly came just looking at her. I knew I would have zipper marks later. And I didn't care.

"I need to touch you," she whispered, and I nodded, taking a step back. Then my phone buzzed.

I cursed as I read the screen. "Fuck. It's an emergency. I have to go."

Livvy stood there, her body flushed, her eyes a little glassy. Before she could answer I slid my fingers into my mouth, tasting her sweetness. Her eyes widened as I reached forward to run those fingers along her lower lip.

"I have to go. But we will finish that. Finish this."

She nodded. "Okay." She let out another breath, her eyes dazed.

So I kissed her again, and made sure she had

what she needed, before going to deal with whatever the hell I had to for this wedding.

Every part of me wanted to be back in that room. Back with Livvy. Deep inside her.

And I knew that even if I had to move mountains, I would find a way to make this work.

Because I did not believe in love at first sight. And yet I had a feeling I was falling right into it anyway.

five
LIVVY

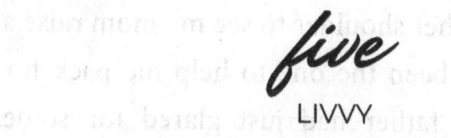

"HAVE YOU SEEN A HORSE?"

My lips twitched, and I nodded at the phone. "Yes. I've seen many horses. And cows."

"Cows?" Amelia's eyes widened comically, and I laughed.

"Yes. They have Angus cows next door, but this ranch has Hereford."

My daughter just blinked at me, and I grinned down at my phone.

"Have your grandpa look it up." I pressed my lips together so I wouldn't laugh at the earnest expression on her face.

Amelia clapped her hands. "Picture?"

"Yes. I will take a photo. I already have a few."

"Where is Ewan?" she asked innocently, while I held back a blush.

I looked over her shoulder to see my mom raise a brow. Mom had been the one to help me pack for this trip, as my father had just glared for some reason. Neither one of them had asked any questions. I would've thought they would have had a million of them considering I did not know this man. My cousin knew him and trusted him implicitly, so that should have been enough. But I had gone on an overnight wedding trip with a man I didn't know, and my mother had packed the damn bag.

And now here my daughter was, asking about him, and my mother continued to smirk.

"He's with the wedding party getting ready for the day. I'll see him later."

Amelia pouted. "He's nice. Is he going to come back? I want to show him my blocks. And cupcakes. I really like cupcakes." She fluttered those eyelashes again, and I barely resisted the urge to narrow my eyes at my mother.

"It's a grandmother's prerogative," Mom said, a bit of shame in her tone.

I held back my playful retort and braced as I turned back to my daughter. "I don't know if I'm going to be able to see him before the wedding. And he lives here, darling. Remember?" I ignored the slightest twinge at that. I knew he lived here. Many *many* miles away from me. This was just an odd dream, an escape.

And I needed to make sure my daughter and I both understood that.

"Tell him hi. And I miss him."

My mother just smiled at me, and I wasn't sure if I saw worry there, or was just projecting it.

I talked to my daughter a few more minutes and held back tears before signing off. I had only slept away from Amelia a handful of nights in my life. She was my purpose. My everything. And leaving her even for a night was difficult. I still couldn't quite believe I had dropped everything and come on this grand adventure. I wasn't sure why I said yes, other than sane me never would have said yes. But I knew I had found myself in some form of rot. Going day by day, hour by hour just trying to survive. I had Amelia, my family, and my job. Thankfully I could work anywhere as long as I had the internet, so jumping on a plane hadn't been that far off in the realm of impossibility. And I had even worked on edits for another book this morning. I scheduled my time enough so I was able to do this, and yet it was still drastically out of character.

As was letting Ewan finger me against the wall. I had never had an orgasm quite like that in my life. And since I hadn't been with anybody since Brick, I had gotten very good at giving myself orgasms. I had the toys and the means to get myself off in many different ways. Because I only had myself to rely on, whether it was my life, my future, or my orgasms.

And yet, Ewan had blown every other experience out of the water.

And just thinking the word blown made me imagine myself on my knees in front of him. If he hadn't been called away, I knew that's where I would've been. I wouldn't care that the hardwood would dig into my knees. I wanted to be down there, his cock in my mouth, and me taking that control. Of course, knowing the rough feel of his calloused hands, perhaps *he'd* be the one in control, guiding himself in and out of my mouth as he wrapped my hair around his fist.

Just thinking about it got me wet. And I knew that was a problem.

Because this weekend was just a temporary moment. An abstract time that would blow up in my face or fade away into memories. Or perhaps both.

Ewan was not forever. I knew that. I didn't want forever. My family could find it. I watched my cousins fall in love. My parents were so damn in love it was quite sickening sometimes. I knew love existed.

I also knew you needed to trust explicitly in order for that to happen.

And I didn't have any trust left in me.

I couldn't even find the man who had been a sperm donor. How the hell was I supposed to trust another?

So perhaps it would be smart for me just to live in the moment. I could protect my heart while having the best sex of my life.

Because I knew it would be the best sex in my life.

Part of me was annoyed he had never come back to the room. I knew it was for a good reason. There had been countless issues that seemed insurmountable for the wedding, and I had been alone in bed, horny as hell, wondering what I was supposed to do.

The whole one room, one bed scenario hadn't been a problem since he hadn't come back at all.

And I wasn't sure how the night was going to go since the wedding would run into the wee hours of the morning most likely. Maybe we wouldn't have time to finish what we had started.

Maybe that single orgasm that made my toes curl

and my knees go weak would have to be enough. And perhaps it would be enough. I would have to make do with the best orgasm of my life. But I wanted more. Just for the night.

And I was never someone who wanted more.

What had this cowboy done to me?

There was a knock at the door, and my shoulders tensed, my thighs pressing together.

It couldn't be Ewan. Could it? He had a key code to the room. But maybe he was giving me privacy.

Or perhaps he was tentative about everything that happened. Maybe he regretted having me come here. It was completely out of the blue, and out of character for him as well from what I could see of his friends and family.

Maybe this was all a complete mistake.

There was another knock, and then someone cleared their throat. "Livvy? Are you in there?"

I scrambled off the bed at the sound of Kandi's voice. Why was the bride at my door on her wedding day? Considering Ewan had left the night before for an emergency, one that he had just said had gotten out of control but hadn't gone into details of, I was worried.

I opened the door quickly as Kandi stood there,

her eyes swollen, her hair on the top of her head, and wearing cut up jeans and a T-shirt.

So unlike what a bride would normally wear.

I immediately did the Montgomery thing and held out my arms for her.

She fell into them, this stranger, and sobbed into my shoulder.

I brought her into the room so that way nobody would see. I didn't know exactly what was going on, but I was not going to let her deal with this on her own and where anyone could watch.

"What's wrong?" I finally asked as Kandi's tears subsided.

"Everything is such a mess." The other woman stood up and wiped her tears, shaking herself a bit.

"I'm so sorry. How can I help?" I could've bitten my tongue by asking that, considering I had no idea what the situation was.

Kandi took a step back and wiped her face. "I'm sorry. I know you don't know me, I'm not always this hyperemotional. I didn't mean for my wedding to be like this, but here we are."

"I've seen my fair share of weddings. It's okay. Just take a breath. Can I get you some water?"

She shook her head. "I have some in the bridal suite. And I'll rehydrate. I even have cheese and crackers, so I have protein and snacks. I thought I was all ready to go. And then I decided to have women I thought I trusted in my bridal party."

I froze, a sense of unease washing over me. "Oh?"

"Did Ewan tell you that he had to deal with an issue last night?"

I nodded, hoping I wasn't blushing too hard at the memory. "But he didn't give me any details."

"Well, Holland ended up with food poisoning. So we were worried it was from the reception dinner, but it turned out she was the *only* one who was sick." Kandi's eyes narrowed. "And it wasn't food poisoning."

It took a moment, and then my eyes widened. "Oh."

"Very much *oh*. And if that wasn't enough, it turns out the baby is Josh's."

I stood in silence for the moment, not really knowing who Josh was. I had seen him across the way when Ewan had pointed the groom's party out, but I didn't know anybody here.

"Oh, I forgot you don't realize all of the soap opera connections in our group. Josh is married to Kendra. And is Sarah's brother."

I quickly tried to do the mental connections. It was something that I was decently good at considering my family. And then I winced. "That does make for complications and poor decisions."

"Exactly. Kendra and Holland got into it, and there was hair pulling and slapping. And Dustin is Holland's brother, and so he and Josh got into it. And then somehow everybody was screaming and fighting, and half of my wedding party is on the outs and kicked off the property."

My stomach fell as I shook my head. "I'm so sorry. I can't even imagine. But today's your day." I hoped I wasn't stepping in it at this point. "I know you had all these plans and you've done so many different related activities with the group. But it is your day with Jackson."

Kandi's smile was brighter than the sun at that moment. "It is. And I love him so much. And I hate all of my friends right now."

I cringed. "I'm sorry about that. I hope you guys can work it out." I paused. "After a lot of time. And preferably not around any sharp objects."

Kandi burst out laughing, and I let out a relieved breath that I hadn't taken it too far. "Ewan said I would like you."

I ignored the warmth spreading through me at that comment.

"Speaking of Ewan, I have a huge favor to ask."

I froze, wondering where she was going with this.

"I know that he asked you here because Trish was annoying him. By the way, Trish is gone. I heard how she talked to you and him, and I'm done. She was my friend from college and in my same sorority. I shouldn't have even had her in my wedding party."

Guilt swamped me. "I'm so sorry. First for crashing your wedding." I let out a hollow laugh. "And for Trish. You did not need to do anything for me. I can handle people like her."

"You shouldn't have to. My wedding was supposed to be happy and bright and cheery. And the people I called friends were not making it that way. I have better friends out there, I promise. I just picked the wrong ones to be close to me on this day. I'm going to figure it out. But I'm going to have Jackson at my side when I do it. Because he's truly the best choice I've ever made."

I smiled at that and reached out, gripping her hand. "See? That's all that matters in a wedding. The person that you are marrying."

Something I would never be doing. But I ignored the odd ache at that.

"You get it. Completely. And Ewan explained the whole fake date thing, but from the way you two are with each other...I don't know if I believe it's that fake."

I pressed my lips together, unsure of what I was supposed to say.

"You don't have to explain. However, I was wondering if you could be my fake bridesmaid?"

I froze, utterly confused, but she continued before I could put my scattered thoughts into words. "Or rather, my fake maid of honor. I'm out of women I trust that are here at the wedding. The women in my life that would normally take this place are stuck in Europe thanks to a weather issue. So I won't even have them here. And I kicked out the people that I thought I trusted. I don't want to say you're my only hope. But you're really my only hope. Ewan's going to be standing up there for Jackson, and I want someone too."

"But I'm a stranger," I said quickly, feeling as though I had lost control of every situation I was currently in.

"You know Ewan. And you might say it's only for a few days, but you guys met at an emotionally heightened situation and bonded. Fate has a silly way of changing things."

I did not want to think about fate when it came to Ewan. Especially because I would be flying home the next day, and I wouldn't see him again. Why did that hurt so much to think about?

"There is no one else you can ask?" I felt desperate here. Tears filled Kandi's eyes again, and I reached out to squeeze her hand once more. "I'm sorry."

"There are other people I could ask, but frankly, I just want a clean slate. And I know that's horrible to ask of you, and a *huge* ask to begin with. But you know Ewan, and the idea of you two walking down the aisle together just makes me happy."

A warning alarm sounded, but I couldn't say anything. Not with the look on her face. "What is it you need me to do?" I asked, and her face brightened.

I had a feeling I had once again leaped off a cliff so high I hadn't been expecting it.

IN THE END, IT HADN'T TAKEN THAT MUCH EFFORT. I had brought a pale pink dress with flowers up the sides, and it turned out it matched the decor enough I didn't have to borrow one of the ill-fated bridesmaids dresses. That wouldn't have been awkward at all. And with the grooms in suit coats and dark jeans, the down-home and yet elegant affair worked.

I knew people would have questions. Namely who the hell I was and how I had been invited to this. However, I wouldn't be the one answering them. Now I stood next to Ewan waiting to go down the aisle, wondering if I could run away.

Ewan's hand reached out, his fingers brushing along my neck.

I held back a shiver, my tongue darting out to lick my lower lip.

His gaze followed the action, and I swallowed hard. "You ready for this?" he asked, that voice a low growl.

"Not even in the slightest. But I've already been out of my comfort zone every moment since I've met you. I might as well continue."

He smirked ever so slightly. I wanted to go on my tiptoes and press my lips against his. But I was already making enough of a scene just being here.

"You look good out of your comfort zone, Livvy Montgomery. I know this is not what you asked for, and hell, I had no idea this is what I would be doing either. But I don't mind being able to walk next to you for a little bit, and then looking at you across the way."

My face flushed, and I shook my head. "I'm going to have to go stand up there in front of one hundred or so people I don't know, so don't get me all hot and bothered."

He leaned down and kissed my bare shoulder. I barely resisted the urge to melt into a puddle.

"Ewan McBride," I warned.

"I like what you say my full name. And by the way, Montgomery, it's more like three hundred."

I nearly pivoted on my heels and ran away, but then the music started, and there was no turning back.

Walking arm in arm with Ewan down the aisle was a surreal experience. The music intensified, and I could feel the stares of others. But Jackson had already announced the change in company, and we were going with it as if it wasn't a big deal.

Going from fake date to fake bridesmaid wasn't on my schedule, but then again, nothing was.

Everything passed in moments, and I stood across the aisle from Ewan, my bouquet and Kandi's in my hands as two people who I just met vowed to love each other until the end of days and beyond. And from the certainty in their voices, I believed it.

No matter the trauma and power surrounding them, trying to take this moment from them, they had persevered. They loved each other. And while I believed in love, sometimes it was hard to see it. Yet not in this moment. Not for these two.

As the wedding blended into the reception, I smiled in Ewan's arms, wondering how I had ended up here once again.

"You look damn beautiful in that dress," Ewan murmured in my ear as we danced pressed up obscenely next to each other.

"I can tell from what's pressing against me," I teased.

"Minx," he growled, biting my earlobe.

I took a step back, grateful for the music change. Climbing him like a tree in public would probably not be a great idea since I was already a spectacle just being there.

"I still can't believe how well people took my presence in the wedding. I expected weird questions and looks, but people are being kind. Curious, but kind."

"You're beautiful, and selfless for being here. Of course they are being kind."

I shook my head, my breath coming quick just staring at him. He was definitely a problem.

"By the way, I noticed how you neatly shuffled to

the side of the dance floor when she threw the bouquet."

I rolled my eyes and shoved at his shoulder playfully as we made our way out of the large tent. People were partying and having a great time, and my part of the festivities was over. Thank God.

"I was already the center of attention far too much. And you didn't catch the garter either."

"I never really understood why that's a thing."

I shrugged. "My cousin looked it up one time, but I don't remember."

"Of course a cousin of yours did."

"Do you think I should figure out what to do with this bouquet?" I asked as I picked up the one I had used for the wedding off our table.

"I forgot to tell you that Kandi said to keep it."

My eyes widened. "Really?"

He gestured toward the numerous tables. "They have hundreds if not thousands of flowers. She wanted you to keep that one. Plus there might be a wedding gift of some sort in the room. I wasn't quite sure exactly what was going on because she was talking quickly and happily. However, the flowers are yours."

My lips formed a smile at that, as I inhaled the

precious blooms. "Amelia will love them. She always wanted to be a flower girl and hasn't had a chance yet. The odds are great she'll be able to one day with one of my cousins or even my brother, so there's hope yet. However, I'll make sure she gets to keep these."

He gave me an odd look, like he was thinking hard, and I had to wonder if he had noticed I had not mentioned my own wedding. But that was far too complicated of a topic for this moment.

"My mom used to dry them a certain way so that way they still kept their form and didn't brown too easily. I can show you. I think Amelia would get a kick out of it."

I sucked in a sharp breath as I nodded in answer. Because he said he was going to teach me. As in he would see me again.

Or maybe it was just a response, and I was thinking too hard.

"I'm really tired," I blurted, knowing I was beyond obvious.

"You know what, so am I. What do you say we make our way back to the room?" He paused. "To get some rest."

I swallowed hard, my knees going weak, and I

practically ran up the path, hoping nobody else noticed.

By the time we were in the room, our breath was coming quick, and I was once again pressed against the door.

"I wanted to rip the dress off of you since I first saw you in it."

"You in those jeans just does something to me. I've never been a jeans person. I always thought suits were the way to go."

"You like me all blue-collar." He leaned forward and bit my bottom lip; the sting nearly sent me over the edge. When he slid his hand up my thigh to grip my ass again, I moaned.

"What is wrong with us? What can't we keep our hands off each other?"

"Did I ask you to stop touching me?" he asked, his voice low.

I kissed him harder in answer.

He picked me up with one arm, and I let out a shocked gasp before wrapping my legs around his waist. He walked toward the bed, and set me down on top of it, hovering over me.

"I need to taste you."

I licked my lips and kicked off my shoes before

letting my legs fall to the side. He smiled like the cat who found the canary as he pushed my dress up over my hips.

"You already soaked your panties. Were you wet all day?"

"I've been on edge since you left me last night," I whispered, my hands cupping my breasts over my dress.

"I will forever hate my friends for pulling me away from you last night. It was all I could do not to lock them in a room together and come back to you so I could fill you up and fuck you until the sun rose. So that's what I'm going to do tonight. I hope you got some sleep last night, because you're not getting any tonight. I'm going to fuck you in every single position possible, until both of us are wrung out, and then go at it again. Are you ready for me? How many times do you think I can make you come?"

I froze, wondering if his words could send me over the edge. Could I come from just words?

And then he pressed his thumb over my clit, and I came.

"One," he growled before whipping my panties off.

I was still coming down from my orgasm as he licked up my slit, and my toes curled. He devoured me, flicking his tongue at my clit and sucking at every inch of me. He bit my thighs and speared into me with two fingers. And when I came again, rocking my pussy against his face, he pulled back, licked his lips, and whispered, "Two."

I sat up and let him strip my dress off me. There had been a built-in bra, so my breasts fell heavy, my nipples so tight at the feel of him. He leaned forward and pressed them between his fingers.

"How the hell did I not realize you were pierced?" he asked, his gaze darkening.

I bit my lip, my fingers playing along the edge of his jeans. "And you still haven't seen all of my tattoos," I whispered.

"Oh, I'm going to lick every single one."

And then he leaned forward and sucked one nipple into his mouth. I arched for him, tugging at his belt.

"I need to see you. It's not fair that I'm naked and you're not."

"We can rectify that," he said with a grin. Then he pulled off his shirt, and my mouth watered. My hands slid up his beautifully tattooed chest, and my nails scraped down his muscled flesh.

"How much ink do you have?"

"Just enough."

"And I'm going to make sure I lick every inch too," I promised.

Ewan wrapped my hair around his fist and pulled my head back. "Good." And then he crushed my mouth to his, and I groaned into him. I pulled down his pants, and he helped me shove them completely off.

When his cock sprung free in front of my mouth, my eyes widened at the barbell piercing at the end.

"You've been hiding things," I teased, lifting the base of his shaft.

He let out a groan, his hand in my hair tightening to the point of pain. But a good pain. "Are you going to be okay with my piercing in your mouth? I don't want you to hurt yourself, or your teeth."

I looked up at him then, pumping him once, twice. "Will you show me how to make it feel good?" I asked, panting.

He let his head fall back, a guttural groan ripping from his throat. "You are the hottest fucking thing I've ever seen in my life."

And then he kissed me again before showing me exactly how he wanted it. He put one hand over mine, shaking. He squeezed himself harder before he gently ran his fingers down my throat.

"That's it, open for me. I'll go slow. I promise."

I licked the tip of his cock and then slowly swallowed him. I hummed along his length, and he shifted his hips slightly, going deeper. When I gagged, he pulled out, but I gripped his hips with my free hand, taking him even deeper. When I swallowed, letting him go past the back of my throat, he began whispering words I couldn't even hear or understand.

When he pulled back, I licked up his shaft. We continued into the moment, testing our desires and strengths. I cupped his balls using one hand and then using my other, I gripped the base of his dick where my mouth couldn't reach. My fingers couldn't even touch around him, and I knew he would stretch me in the best ways possible soon.

I continued to go down on him, loving the noises he made. When he pulled out, I frowned up at him, my lips swollen, my breasts heavy.

"As much as I want to come down that pretty throat or on those gorgeous tits, I really need to fuck you now."

I nodded eagerly as I leaned back. "Finally!"

We both laughed, and then he reached into the nightstand to pull out an entire box of condoms.

My eyes widened, and he just grinned. "I told you it's going to be a long night."

I helped him sheath himself, and both of us shook as we did so, the momentum and anticipation twining in a way that had never happened before in my life. And then he was hovering over me, settling between my thighs, and I reached up to push his hair back from his face.

He smiled down at me, and kissed me softly, a gentleness that we hadn't had before, or at least not since that first time.

For some reason tears pricked my eyes, but I blinked them away as he looked down at me.

"Are you ready?" he asked, his voice strained.

"Yes, always."

And then he smiled before plunging deep. The intrusion was almost too much, his cock thick and long. I let out a shocked gasp as he froze deep inside me, not even fully seated.

"Did I hurt you?"

My fingernails dug into his shoulders, but I shook my head. "No, it has been a really long time."

We met gazes, and that's when I knew he understood. He swallowed hard before pulling out gently, then inching deep inside me. I moved my hands to grip him around his hips and pulled him in deeper.

"Save gentle for later. I want you however you can have me now," I panted.

His eyebrows scrunched as if he wasn't sure if I was telling the truth, so I lifted my hips, meeting his thrust. And when I slid my fingers between the globes of his ass and played with him there, he rolled his eyes back before he moved.

He pounded into me, and I met him thrust for thrust, needing him. He pulled out of me, a growl escaping his throat as he flipped me on my hands and knees and continued to pound into me. I couldn't breathe, couldn't think, but with each motion, I was sent closer and closer to the edge. I crawled up the headboard, angling my back so he could go deeper, and with one hand on my hip, he slid the other to cup my breast and play with the piercing there.

I came again, clamping around his cock, and he leaned forward to bite down on my shoulder.

I moaned, using one hand to play with my clit, as he continued to move, both of us panting. When he finally came, he held me so close to him, I couldn't tell where he began and I ended, but it didn't matter. This moment would be etched in my memory for all time.

Because it had been the hardest, hottest sex of my life, and yet, the most delicate.

And later, after he cleaned me up, he licked every

inch of me again, feasting on me as if I were only his. And then we did indeed find every position possible in that small room where the single bed proved to be barely sturdy enough to take us.

And as we caught our breaths while clinging to each other, I told myself I would be able to walk away.

I had to.

The sun rose over the mountains, the spears of light sliding through the blinds, as he kissed me softly, entering me from behind.

I was sore and tired, but I couldn't stop moving.

"That's it, take me. One last time."

Last.

"I lost count," I muttered, out of energy, yet it felt as if lightning bounced around inside me.

"I didn't," he said cockily.

And I finally came, this time knowing he did with me.

"I don't want this to end," he whispered after moments, and I froze, afraid of what he would say. But what could either of us say?

"You can tell me no. You can tell me to go. But I don't want this to be our only night."

"You. My family—"

"We will figure it out. I'll go with you though. Back to Colorado. I'm figuring things out."

I let the tears fall as I nodded, knowing that nothing good could come from this.

But I didn't want to let go either.

Even if it broke me in the end.

six
EWAN

THOUGH MY BROTHERS had given me shit, taking time off for the first time in history was actually good thing. My sister had been the one to practically kick me out of the house, telling me that if I came back without seeing what the hell this meant with Livvy, she would change the locks. Frankly, I wouldn't be surprised if she'd changed the locks anyway. Just to be contrary.

My small town of Clover Lake was my home. It was my blood. But Livvy already meant so much more.

And although Livvy probably thought my desire to go back with her to Colorado had been in the heat of the moment, I had been thinking about it ever since the plane ride to Wyoming.

And thought about it again at the rehearsal.

And again at the wedding.

And again when I had been deep inside her.

I had never had that kind of connection with another human being in my life, and it only marginally had to do with sex. No, most of it had everything to do with the woman currently dancing in the kitchen.

I leaned against the doorway and watched as she shook that luscious ass of hers back and forth, making Amelia giggle.

Amelia mimicked the motion, wiggling her butt in jerky motions, and grinned up at her mother.

The two of them were baking cookies, something that Livvy didn't get to do often, but she had finished her work early, taking the time to dance with her daughter, while I stood back and watched, trying to soak in every moment.

It had been three weeks since I had flown down to Colorado with her, and I didn't know when I was going home. I knew I needed to soon. My life and my ranch were up north. I was still handling a lot of paperwork and computer work from Livvy's, and my brothers were grateful for that because that meant they didn't have to do it.

I missed the land. I wasn't too edgy to be in the

city like this—after all, I could still see the mountains and it wasn't like we were in high-rises. But I missed my small town. Only I knew I could walk away if I had to. That surprised me. I hadn't known this family long enough to walk away from my life, but I would. Because I loved that woman in the kitchen. And I loved that little girl staring up at her mom with a bright smile on her face.

I didn't know when it happened, or how, but I was in love with both of them. I would destroy the earth to protect that little girl. And I had no idea where that urge came from. Part of me always knew I would be a father. It just felt like something I would do. I'd find a woman, get married, have kids. Continue to do what my family had done for generations on our land.

Yet I had never pictured something like *this*.

I didn't want anything different.

I didn't want to get attached. I hadn't wanted anything like this at all.

And yet there was no way I couldn't be attached to this family.

Lex and Crew hadn't said a damn thing about me coming back with Livvy. And that probably should've worried me more than anything. Because if they thought this was a done deal, then maybe I was in over my head. Or they thought I would leave and would kick my ass before they had to pick up the pieces I left behind.

And I did not want to hurt the women in front of me.

I wasn't staying at the house, though part of me wanted to. I was staying at one of the Montgomery rentals nearby and was a little alarmed at the conglomerate the family had started to maintain. But I wasn't going to look too deeply into it. I had a place to stay that wasn't underneath the same roof as Amelia. Which made it harder for me to spend as much time with Livvy as I wanted. However it also saved my ass because I was pretty sure Livvy's father and uncles would have a few words to say if I had moved in.

I swallowed hard at the notion. No, not moving in. I was figuring shit out. I wasn't going to overthink things or go too quickly.

Even though I was doing exactly that in both cases.

"Ewan!" Amelia ran to me and jumped. I held out my arms and caught her in midair, surprised at how much trust she put in that action. Livvy didn't look too shocked at that, so maybe Amelia jumped into all of her family's arms. But it warmed me deep inside that Amelia would trust me that way.

I put her on my hip and tapped her nose with my finger.

"Hello, Amelia. Are you making cookies?"

"I like cookie dough."

I wiped cookie dough off her cheek and nodded. "I can see that. Cookie dough is my favorite too." I leaned forward and whispered loudly, "Don't tell your mom, but I think I might like dough more than cookies."

"I won't tell." Amelia grinned at me, and my heart caught.

Livvy rolled her eyes. "You two are a menace. However, we are having fun with these cookies. These are thumbprints."

My stomach rumbled. "My mom makes those with the jam from some of the fruit she has on the ranch. I'm very spoiled."

"Yes, you are. And I did make the strawberry jam. The strawberries I bought from the local store." She winked as she said it, and I leaned down and brushed my lips against hers.

Amelia clapped and kissed my cheek, and Livvy just grinned.

Kissing in front of Amelia was a relatively new

thing. But again, everything about this situation was new. But we didn't know how much longer I would be able to stay, and we had been very good about not talking about that. Meaning hiding everything from Amelia just couldn't happen.

I just hoped I didn't hurt either of them in the end.

"You make your own jam?" I asked, pushing away worries and doubts because I needed to live in the moment.

Livvy studied my face, as if she had heard my thoughts. "Not always, but I was feeling a little energetic."

I raised a brow at her, knowing exactly why she felt energetic, and she rolled her eyes at me.

"Well, do you need a taste tester? I feel like you need a taste tester."

"I want to taste! I want to taste!" Amelia said as she clapped her hands against my cheeks. I winced ever so slightly because I had no idea why her hands were so sticky. I knew the running joke between my friends with children that they always had jam hands, but I hadn't truly lived it until this moment.

"Okay, let's get you both washed up," Livvy said with a laugh. I carried Amelia to the sink, and we washed her hands, her face, and then my face.

"I like your beard," Amelia said as she patted at my face.

"I wonder what you look like with the beard," I said softly.

Amelia's eyes widened and she put her hands on her cheeks. "Oh no. No beard for me."

"You never know, one day you just end up with car tweezers though." I looked over at Livvy, who shrugged. "There's always a hidden chin hair. And you can only see it in the light through your car windshield."

"These are things I do not know."

"I guess you're learning everything."

My heart lurched again, wanting to know everything but not sure when the end would come.

As we finished up the cookies, and started on dinner, I couldn't help but relish in the domesticity of it. Amelia always had family around her, and Livvy was supported. Yes, her job meant that she could work anywhere, but her family was here. She was *happy* here.

I could leave Wyoming. Maybe fly back often to help out when needed during high seasons, but I could find something to do here.

I had fallen in love with this family, and it meant

I would do anything to figure out a way to make it work.

By the end of the evening we found ourselves sitting on Livvy's porch, rocking on the wooden bench one of her uncles had made. Amelia sat between us, talking a million miles a minute about one of her cousins.

I wrapped my arm behind Livvy's shoulders and played with her hair as the sun began to set, and things just felt right.

Tonight. Tonight I would tell Livvy I loved her. And that I would do all I could to make sure I did not fuck things up for her family. I didn't have any answers, other than I needed to find those answers.

A car pulled into the driveway, and Livvy frowned.

"Who is it, Mommy?" Amelia asked, leaning forward.

Unease settled over me as Livvy stood up and walked toward the man getting out of the truck.

I recognized him as one of the Montgomerys, but I didn't remember which. Amelia tried to wiggle off the seat, so I stood up and took her with me. For some reason, everything felt off about this, so I put Amelia on my hip again, and lifted my chin at the other man.

"Hey. I'm Noah. I don't know if you remember me."

Another car pulled in beside Noah, and fear coated my tongue. Shep and Shea Montgomery got out of their SUV, and ice filled my veins. If everybody was coming here unannounced, something was wrong.

"Grandma! Grandpa!" Amelia wiggled down my body, oblivious to the tension, and ran toward her grandparents.

Shep lifted his granddaughter up and nodded at me.

"Hey Amelia, darling, let's go inside. I really want some lemonade. Do you have any?"

"I do. I do."

Shea leaned forward to kiss her granddaughter's cheek before squeezing Livvy's hand. "We'll be right inside."

There was something wrong, something they needed to protect Amelia from, and I wanted everybody to leave. Whatever perfect moment we had been enjoying was shattered, and there was no going back. I did not want to know what Noah had to say. Only I knew I wasn't going to have a choice.

"What is it, Noah? Who's hurt?"

Noah gave me a look before moving forward and holding Livvy's hands.

"The family is safe. We're all okay and I need you to breathe." He swallowed hard. "I found Brick, Livvy."

I moved toward Livvy in an instant, putting my hand on her shoulder for comfort.

"Why are you saying it like that? Does he want Amelia? Oh my God. Should you get a lawyer? Will his family be doing the same?"

Noah's face went gray, and I knew that it wasn't anything like her vivid nightmares. But somehow it was worse.

"Brick died six months ago, Livvy. Car accident. He didn't have ID on him at the time, so he was a John Doe for a long while. I don't have all the information yet, but I'll get it. But Brick is gone, Livvy. I'm sorry."

Livvy stiffened under my hand, and I squeezed her shoulder. I didn't say anything, there wasn't much to say. I knew that Livvy did not love Brick. She had never loved him. But he was still her daughter's father. And she had cared for him at one point.

"Thank you for telling me," Livvy said, her voice wavering. I met Noah's gaze, his worry matching mine.

"Do you want to go inside? We can talk."

Livvy shook her head. "No. It's good there was some resolution. I don't know. I should go and make sure Amelia is doing well. Thank you, Noah."

And then she turned on her heel, and walked away, leaving me behind with Noah.

"I'm sorry, Ewan. I don't know what to do. She's always been the one who closes herself off the most from us. She's going to break soon, and I don't know how to fix that. That means I'm going to be the asshole who leaves this on your shoulders."

"I've got big shoulders. I'll be here." It was a promise I hoped I could keep. Because from the way Livvy had looked at me in that instant, I didn't know if she wanted me to be there for her. And that thought scared me more than anything.

Noah studied my face before giving me a tight nod. "I believe you. I'm glad she has you."

Did she? It wasn't feeling like it at the moment.

"I guess I should go inside. Hell, I don't know what to say."

"I don't think she's going to want to see me. At least for a little bit. I've been trying to find the man for years. Turns out I was too late."

Before I could say anything in response, Noah

hopped in his truck and left, leaving me standing there with my hands in my pockets, wondering what the hell I was supposed to say.

I stood there in the sunset, knowing I couldn't do nothing for much longer. As I made my way inside, both of the older Montgomerys gave me a worried looks but didn't say anything.

I watched as Livvy went through the nighttime routine, without saying a word to her parents or me, and pretended everything was okay. Even though it clearly wasn't.

And when Shep and Shea left, both giving me pleading glances, I stood in the doorway as Livvy tucked in her daughter.

"Will you tuck me in, Mr. Ewan?" she asked, her voice so small, so sweet.

Livvy stiffened, her jaw tightening, and I knew I should probably say no. To not tie myself anymore to this family, but I couldn't say no to that little girl.

I moved forward to finish tucking in Amelia, and then kissed the top of her head.

"Good night, Amelia. Sleep well, lovebug."

"I love you, Mr. Ewan."

It was like a kick to the gut, and I felt more than saw Livvy go straight next to me.

But I couldn't break this little girl's heart. So I brushed her hair from her face and smiled down. "I love you too, Amelia," I whispered. Then I swallowed hard and took a step back, leaving her and Livvy alone.

I found myself in the kitchen again, wondering if I could pour myself a drink. I had no idea what I was doing. I couldn't help. Not when I knew Livvy needed to have a hard conversation with her daughter, and I would just be in the way. Because every time I looked at Livvy, she was pulling away. Any control or ideas I had were slipping through my fingers like sand.

Livvy came out a few moments later, and I turned to see her staring at me, her eyes slightly vacant.

I moved forward then, knowing if I didn't hold her, I would never be able to again. So I cupped her face, and she leaned into my palm.

"I'm so damn sorry, Livvy."

"I don't know how to tell her. I need to. One day. Not now, but one day. It's going to confuse her." She paused and stared into my eyes. And in that moment, I knew I needed to be the stronger person. Because if I pushed right now, she would break. And if I pushed, I would hurt Amelia. Livvy gave me a watery smile. "I don't want to be the person that falls into mistakes because I'm scared. Because I'm reaching out. I don't know what to do, Ewan. But I can't hurt her."

It was like another kick, a slice. But the sad part was I understood. We had only been in each other's lives for less than a month. And that little girl already told me she loved me. And now her world was going to shatter when she heard about her daddy. And I wasn't part of that. Even if I had rushed far too quickly into feelings I'd never had before.

"I should go," I said into the silence, my voice just as hollow as hers.

Because I didn't want to be her mistake.

Livvy didn't correct me. Didn't beg me to stay. "I've already hurt her once. I'm afraid if I take a chance on something that we have no answers for, I'll hurt her even more."

"That might be true. You could. But you're also afraid for yourself." She winced, and I cursed myself for saying the words. But they needed to be out there. "So I'll go. But just know, if you'd have asked me, I'd have found a way to stay." And I leaned forward, brushing my lips against hers, a goodbye so bitter it coated my tongue.

And then I walked away, leaving the family I loved behind me.

Because Livvy wasn't ready for me to fight for her. But when she was, I'd have to find a way to be there. Even if there was nothing left of me.

seven

LIVVY

GRIEF WAS SUCH AN ODD THING. It was never constant, nor did it truly make sense. I hadn't loved Brick. I perhaps at one point thought I had loved him—could love him. The same way I had loved the idea of who we could be together. Or the fact that my daughter had come from our time together. So I did not know why Brick's death hit me like this.

Crushing waves of uncertainty and helplessness.

It felt as if somebody carved out part of my soul and would never give it back.

"Can I get you tea? Anything?"

I looked into the hollow gaze of my cousin and best friend, and almost asked her the same thing. She had secrets of her own and wasn't saying anything. I couldn't tell what was wrong, or how to fix this.

Then again, I was in similar quicksand.

"I'm okay. Thank you."

Aria gave me a look, and then glanced down at the tattered up napkin in my hand. I hadn't even realized I had torn it into so many pieces.

"Okay, perhaps I'm not fine or okay. But I will be. I just know that one day my little girl is going to grow up and I'm going to have to tell her what happened to her dad."

Amelia was too young to understand now, so I was given the reprieve of not having to explain. Although part of me knew it wasn't quite a reprieve. As everything hurt so much. I was afraid waiting would just intensify it over time.

"I realize you are upset that Brick is dead because a man is dead. But that's not why you're acting like this."

I blinked at her, utterly confused. "What on earth are you talking about?"

She raised a brow at me. "Where is Ewan, Livvy?"

I froze, not having heard his name since he had left. I still couldn't quite believe that he had just walked out of the house, never to return. Yes, he had needed to. This wasn't his home. But he was gone.

And I had forced him out. I didn't fight for him, nor did I say I wanted him in the slightest. So why would he have stayed?

"I can't. I can't talk about him."

"I know you're scared. Scared of what could happen to you and Amelia if it doesn't work out with Ewan. But I saw the way you guys are together. That type of chemistry is one in a million. It doesn't just happen every day. It might have felt too fast, too intense, but it was something."

"And he left," I whispered, my voice cracking.

"Because you needed him to."

Why did I understand and hate that statement? "It's another mistake. I thought I could trust Brick. I was wrong."

"You were young and Brick and Ewan aren't even in the same stratosphere when comparing the two. You and I both know that."

"But Ewan's whole life is up north. He lives on a ranch in Wyoming. Clover Lake is a small town and his family and Jackson's practically run the place. It's *their* place. And I don't think it's something meant for a Montgomery."

"Well, to start with, long distance relationships can work for a little while. It gives you time to sort things out."

I shook my head. "That wouldn't be fair to Amelia."

Aria winced. "I realize you have a support system here, but that family has a private jet." My cousin rolled her eyes. "Which is insane to me, but I'm off-topic here. It's not *that* far. Even driving it's not that far. Yes, your family is here, but you know damn well I would be up at that ranch to visit you as much as possible. Clover Lake sounds adorable and in need of a Montgomery. I mean, every small town is in need of a Montgomery. You told me he said that he would've found a way to stay. And I believe that. But your job is easier to move. Hell, I wouldn't be surprised if we build a Montgomery home in Wyoming just to be closer to you and Amelia. You know us, we sort of take over the world."

I let out a watery laugh and shook my head. "Three days. It's been three days and I miss him so much. It's ridiculous. I barely even know him."

"These weeks have been the most intense, and you *do* know him. Take it from me, watching the person that you crave and are perfect for walk away tears your soul right out of your body, and there's no coming back from that. I know it's not going to be easy. And it's going to come with obstacles that no one is prepared for, but at least one of us should have a happy ending, right?" She blinked away tears.

"Aria, what's wrong?"

She shook her head, rubbing her hands over her face. "This is not about me. I realize I circled toward my own problems, but this is about you. If you want Ewan, you should *try*. Don't walk away because you're scared of what happened with Brick. That man doesn't matter. And I know I'm going to hell for speaking ill of the dead, but he was never here, Livvy. The part of him that mattered in this life of ours died long ago. It's not fair that life is too short but it's also not fair that he left you scrambling. Yes, you got Amelia out of the deal, but that's the only good thing that matters."

I reached out and squeezed her hand. "I don't want to confuse her."

Aria gave me a sad smile. "Take time to talk it out. Figure things out. I know you can."

"But what if Ewan doesn't want this?"

"But what if he does?"

"Mommy!" I whirled as Amelia came running toward me and stopped quickly right in front of the couch where Aria and I sat.

"What's wrong, baby girl?" I asked, searching her face for glimpses of Brick. Only I can't find anything.

She looked so much like a Montgomery, so much just Amelia, that I couldn't see the man who was half of her genes. But he had been zero part of her life. One day I would have to talk to her. One day she would have to know exactly what happened.

But not today.

"I drew a picture of the flowers Mr. Ewan gave me. But I want to draw a horse. I'm not good at it but he said he would help me. When is he coming back?"

Aria gave me a look, and I ignored her even as my pulse raced. "Mr. Ewan went home, Amelia. He lives far away."

Amelia's face fell. "But I love him. He's growly and smiles. And he tickles me with his beard. And he tucks me in. And he loves me too. Why can't I see him?" she pouted, and I blinked away tears, wondering how I could've made so many mistakes. I had tried to protect Amelia, just like I tried to do the same for my heart. And I had failed utterly in both cases.

I had lost something I hadn't even realized I had held, and I needed to fix this.

"Mr. Ewan is such a good man, isn't he?" I asked, my voice soft.

"The best." Amelia nodded enthusiastically. "I want to see him again. When?"

"I don't know, baby."

Tears fell down my daughter's cheeks, and I pulled her into a hug, my own tears following.

"I want to see Mr. Ewan. Please? Can we visit? Can he come here? I love him."

I could hear Aria sniffling next to me as I pulled Amelia into my lap and rocked her.

"I'll fix this, Amelia. I'm going to try, okay?"

"And will he stay here like before? Or can we go there?" Her eyes widened. "We can bring Grandma and Grandpa and see the horses."

"Do you like the horses or Mr. Ewan?" Aria teased.

Amelia gave us a very serious look. "Both. I love both. But I love Mr. Ewan more."

And with that, I promptly burst into tears, and my daughter gave me a startled look, her tiny eyebrows shooting up, before trying to wipe them away.

"I will go find him. I promise." And I'd figure out what the hell I was doing next at some point.

"Good." She gave me an adorably pompous nod. "Because I miss him."

I looked at Aria over my daughter's head and saw

the longing there. My cousin was in pain, and I could fix this.

But maybe I could fix what I had done to my own family.

I just had to hope I wasn't making yet another mistake.

THE FLIGHT TO WYOMING TOOK LONGER WHEN I HAD to fly commercial, and there wasn't a direct flight to the small town where Ewan's family resided. I rented a car and doubted myself with every passing mile. Amelia hummed in the back seat and looked so excited and worried at the same time, that I had questioned my decision countless times. My parents had dropped us off at the airport, apprehension and something I couldn't read etched on their faces. But then my father had practically shoved me out of the SUV when they'd dropped us off.

"I almost made the worst mistake of my life by nearly letting your mother walk away. I know there aren't any easy answers, but I saw the way he treats you and my granddaughter. I was getting the feeling if you didn't go there, he'd be back here soon."

My eyes had widened. "How could you know that?"

"Because he's a good man."

So there I was, driving to the McBride ranch, hoping I wasn't making a mistake.

I should have warned him, should have called, but it would've given me distance to the point I wasn't sure I would be able to make the choices I needed to.

And frankly, I needed to see him.

I tapped in the code to the gate, aware it was odd that I even had it. But he had mentioned it to me in passing, because in that short amount of the time, we had clicked.

And I had almost let it all slip away. I wasn't going to do it again.

I drove down the road, taking in everything at once. This place was beautiful. The mountains in the distance, the farmland and animals everywhere. I knew that the working part of the ranch was a few miles down at a different entrance, but this gate was just for the land Ewan owned. I had directions to his house, and I had hoped he was there. Maybe he was working. Maybe I was about to drive up to a completely empty house, or one filled with people I didn't know. Or maybe Ewan had already found someone else. "It hasn't been that long. Get a grip, Livvy."

"Are we here? Are we here?"

I looked in the rearview mirror at my daughter, knowing that no matter what happened, she would remember this moment. She might have been too young at the moment but bringing my daughter to the ranch she couldn't stop talking about had been the only choice.

"We are. We just have to hope he's home."

I probably *should* have called ahead. Surprising Ewan with not only myself, but my four-year-old daughter, was ridiculous. And yet, here I was. With no way to turn around and change my mind. Hence why we were doing it like this. I couldn't let any more doubt creep in.

I finally pulled in front of a large two-story home that felt as if it was pulled directly from my dreams. A large front porch, and a balcony that looked to be directly from the master bedroom as Ewan had said. Everything looked welcoming, and far too big for a single man.

Once again, I was making impromptu decisions and wondering if I made mistakes. But no, this felt right.

Finally. This felt right.

Before I could even stop the car, the front door opened, and my heart leapt into my throat.

"Mr. Ewan!" Amelia called, kicking her feet in her seat.

He stood there, hands on hips as he stared at me, his face going pale. He had on a flannel shirt buttoned over a white undershirt and those tight jeans I loved so much.

"I want to get out. I want to get out." I heard Amelia trying to work her way out of her booster and seatbelt, and I finally turned off the car.

"Okay, give me a moment."

And then Ewan was running down the front steps as I threw myself out of the car.

"You're here!" He gasped.

I looked up at him, staring into his gorgeous gray eyes. He hadn't changed at all since I had last seen him. That made sense since it hadn't been that long. But it felt as if it had been ages.

A lifetime.

"I am."

He cupped my face, brushing my hair back. "And you brought the kid," he said, letting out a rough chuckle as if he couldn't quite believe it. Frankly I couldn't either.

"Mr. Ewan! I'm here!"

"I see that, Ames." He stared at me then, shaking his head. "You came."

I cleared my throat. "We should probably get Amelia out of the backseat before she gnaws through the door."

Ewan threw his head back and laughed, and then we moved around the car to let Amelia out. She threw herself into his arms, and as he clutched her to his chest, holding the back of her little head with his large hand, my heart squeezed. It felt as if a rope pulled around my chest and soul, tying it up into this moment, this perfection, this love.

"I've missed you, Ames," Ewan whispered as he rocked my daughter back and forth.

I had expected Amelia to start talking a million miles a minute about horses and missing him, but instead her little shoulders were shaking as she sobbed into his neck.

"Don't go. I missed you."

Ewan opened his watery eyes and looked over at me. "I've got you, Amelia. You're going to be okay."

When Ewan shifted to move his other arm, I went to his side, clinging to him. He held Amelia on one hip as he kissed the top of my head, a slightly chaotic laugh abruptly coming from my chest.

"I know I should have called, but that would have given me an excuse not to come."

"I'm glad you're here, Livvy." He looked over at my daughter. "You too, Amelia."

I let out a shaky breath. "I know we have a lot to talk about, a lot to do with what's next. But we wanted to see you."

"And horses."

Ewan grinned so widely, I fell in love once again in his arms. "We can do that." He looked into my eyes again, his face serious. "I'd have come back. I was just here trying to figure out how to make it work. Because walking away from you was the hardest thing I have ever done." He paused. "And the most moronic."

I gave a rough laugh as I reached out to cup his bearded cheek. "I don't know what we have in store, or what will happen next, but I'm here."

"Just let me love you," he whispered against my lips, and I nodded.

"As long as you teach me how to do it, because I'm so afraid I'll mess this up. I'm so scared by how much I love you."

"Well it's a good thing we have time to figure it out."

And then he kissed me, and I couldn't think of

much else—even as Amelia clapped beside us in Ewan's arms.

"I can't wait to introduce you to my family, because I'm pretty sure they think I made you up."

I tensed, even though I was excited. "I should warn you that the Montgomerys will be here en masse. Mostly because they can't stay away."

Laughter danced in his eyes. "Thankfully we have the acreage. At least I hope so."

Then he walked us into his home, and we took the next steps into whatever future we carved out for ourselves.

Even if it was too swift, too outrageous, too scary. It was all too real, and exactly what we needed.

If you'd like to read a bonus scene featuring Livvy and Ewan, you can find it HERE.

Don't worry, Ewan's secretive family are each getting their own romance in the Clover Lake series. Make sure you're signed up for preorder alerts for when the next book is announced! Yay!

Shep & Shae's romance, Ink Inspired, started it all. So don't miss out Livvy's parents fell in love in New Orleans!

Lexington Montgomery finds his match in Last Chance Seduction in the Montgomery Ink Legacy series! Livvy and Ewan are also part of that series and will make guest appearances.

bonus epilogue
LIVVY

"MONTGOMERY COWBOYS. WHAT DO YOU THINK?"

I looked over at my brother and shook my head. "I don't really think that's a thing."

"It's totally a thing. Or at least, it *could* be. You've been here in Clover Lake for months now so you've got the lay of the land. Mom and Dad always said we could reach for the stars. One of us could be president. The other a rocket scientist."

"We already have a rocket scientist in the family," I cut in.

John rolled his eyes. "Fine. We can scratch that one off the list. But we do not have any Montgomery cowboys yet. I looked at the spread. It could be a thing."

"Did you just say spread?" I asked, barely resisting the urge to laugh.

"I would look good with a cowboy hat. I'm just saying."

"You know, they do have ranches in Colorado. The entire state isn't merely I10 with cities popping up all over it. There's an entire east and south Colorado. You should visit it sometime."

I tilted my face up to Ewan as he walked over to us, my heart beating so loudly I was afraid my family would be able to hear it across the clearing.

Ewan gave me a certain small smile telling me far more than anything he could ever say, and I nearly sighed into him. When he lowered his hand and gently ran it against my cheek, I let out an audible sigh.

"Well, it looks like I'm clearly in the way," John said with a clearing of his throat. "And if you're not going to let me be a Montgomery cowboy in Clover Lake, Wyoming, I suppose I will have to make it work in Colorado. Maybe I can go down to the rodeo, see a barrel racer. Barrel racers are hot."

I threw my pen at him, and John barely caught it with those catlike reflexes before running toward my parents who currently had Amelia in their arms.

I shook my head again and looked back at Ewan,

who only had eyes for me. It was so odd to think I knew exactly what was on his mind in that moment. *Me.*

I had never been the center of anyone's attention before. At least, not purely. I had always shared that spot. And I hadn't minded as a daughter, sister, a cousin. Sharing that spotlight was what made a family healthy.

No, I had never felt like this with anyone else in my life. Because I had never been loved like this. I was the center of humans in this moment.

Could freely melt into a puddle.

When he lowered his head, brushing his lips against my own, I nearly swooned.

And I, Livvy Montgomery, did not swoon.

"I'm fucking happy that you're here."

That deep voice of his went straight to my soul.

I patted the steps next to me. "Join me. Because I'm glad that I'm here as well."

When I had been younger, watching the truly independent women in my life, I promised myself I would never pack everything up, throw away what didn't work, and change my life completely for a man. I was going to be that independent woman who stood up for herself and didn't compromise.

And how idiotic it would have been if I had truly leaned into that mindset.

Because that was not how my parents lived. Yes, my mother had moved from New Orleans to Colorado where my father's family was from, but it wasn't that she had been torn from it. She had freely left that city and all of its painful memories behind. All to start new *together*. They had made compromises with each other. Just like the majority of my family who'd found each other later.

I had been so scared because of what Brick had done, that I hadn't even realized I had built those walls around myself. And not merely around my heart, but my life, and my daughter as well.

Somehow this cowboy had climbed over that wall and had thrown me a rope. He had tossed me over his shoulder and taken me away. Then he had knocked down that wall. He had given me a new direction. One where I could take his hand, or I could walk away.

And I was never going to walk away from Ewan McBride.

Ewan took the seat next to me and sighed as I stared at the worn jeans that hugged his ass. I realized that a man in Wranglers could do that to a woman.

"I see you checking me out."

I could feel the heat rising to my skin, but instead of hiding from it, I just looked him up and down and winked.

"I can't help it. You're kind of hot."

"You're going to make me blush, Montgomery."

I snorted and leaned forward, resting my forehead against his. "You should be careful about calling me Montgomery. There are a few of us here."

"That there is. How many more did you say are coming this week?"

I held back a smile at the hesitation and slight worry in his tone.

"My entire family is not coming here right now. Do not worry. Just some of my favorite cousins, the ones that you've met and are currently friends with will be visiting. They just had a few things to deal with." I tried not to think about that too hard because I knew a couple of cousins might not be able to make an appearance at all.

They had far more in their lives to overcome then I had ever thought possible, but they would have me to rely on. Even if I was far away.

"First, when we say some of your favorite cousins, that means all of them. Because I know you actually like your family." I opened my mouth to speak, but Ewan slipped his finger over my lips. I melted, and he just smiled that beautiful smile of his. "Second, why did you get those shadows in your eyes just then? You were overthinking as it was before I sat down next to you. Talk to me."

I sighed, wondering how he could know me so well. Then again hadn't I just thought of my own surprise that I could read him just as well?

"I'm worried about a few of them, but you know why." I didn't keep secrets from Ewan, nor did he with me. And we were still learning each other with each passing day. "I do love my family equally, but I do have a list of favorites. It's what you have to do to enjoy yourself."

"So you're saying I should make a list of my favorite people in your family?"

"Please do," I said with a laugh, and he leaned down, kissing me softly.

I was never going to get used to that.

His touch. His taste.

The way that I knew his gaze would dart over to the side every so often just like mine did to ensure Amelia was okay.

This man loved my baby girl just as much as I did.

And just like that, my heart broke open into a

thousand pieces, to ensure that I could wrap it around Ewan.

"Livvy. Talk to me."

Again, that deep voice just did something to me.

"I am thinking about how blessed I am." His eyes widened marginally in surprise. "I never expected you. Honestly, I never thought to even try dreaming someone like you up."

He pushed my hair back from my face, and he swallowed hard. "I never tried to dream you up either. However, asking you to be my fake date to a wedding where everybody already knew there was no way you could be one, in truth, was kind of genius." His eyes crinkled at the side as he smiled.

I leaned forward to kiss his chin. "I am your date from here on out, at least. So that worked. And at the next wedding, I can plan ahead."

"What if that wedding was ours?" he asked softly.

I froze, leaning backward, my heart racing. "Excuse me?

"Don't sound so surprised, Montgomery."

"Ewan," I whispered, tears threatening as my whole world lit up with this man's words.

He leaned forward and brushed his lips against mine. "What did you think I was going to ask you, Livvy? I love you from the very depths of my soul. I couldn't keep my eyes off you the first time I saw you in the park, and I will be forever grateful that I was there."

My heart beat quickly, and I swallowed hard. "You saved my baby girl."

"You saved *me*."

"I hardly think those two equate to each other."

"We can disagree on that. You wrapped your soul around mine, just like I want to do the same to yours. You came up to Wyoming and brought that little girl I love so much with you. I want to be yours in truth, Livvy. You traveled so far to be here, and I want to make sure you know I'm yours. And I'll do everything in my power to make sure you never regret it."

Tears fell down my cheeks as I tried to catch my breath. "You're our home too, Ewan."

Ewan kissed my tears away. "And if you ever want to visit your family, we have a plane to get you there."

"That still sounds unbelievable." I paused. "Should I ask how rich you are?" I teased, loving the way he threw his head back and laughed.

"I like how you're asking that before you answer my question. Smart."

I slid my hands over my face, mortification settling in. "That's not what I meant."

"I know, Liv. I know. Now, what do you say? You said yes to being my fake date, will you be my real wife?"

I looked down, and my breath caught in my throat.

He held an old-fashioned ring with a large oval diamond in the center, and more diamonds and blue gems surrounding the center stone.

"It's beautiful," I whispered

My tough cowboy cleared his throat. "It was my grandmother's. She had dainty hands just like you. Hopefully it fits."

"I don't even know what to say..."

"Marry me. We already promised to live our lives together. Here on the ranch, and down south with all of the Montgomerys. So no matter what happens, I am going to spend the rest of my life with you. But I want to do it as your husband. I want to face the future together, knowing that we have balance between us. Call me old-fashioned, but watching my best friend say his vows to the love of his life made me realize I want to do the same."

"I never thought I would get married," I whispered, speaking my biggest fear.

"Because the men in Denver and Colorado Springs are the most selfish asinine people I've ever met." He burst out laughing, and he just shook his head at me. "You should have been taken long ago."

"Maybe I was waiting for you? Or maybe I felt old-fashioned."

"Let's figure this journey out together. Let me help you raise that baby girl who captured my heart right along with you. You've been living up here for a few months now. I want you to stay. I might even let you convince me to change my name."

"I think we can find a compromise." I let out a breath and watched as he slid the ring onto my finger. "Yes. I will marry you. And I cannot wait to figure this out with you."

Tears were sliding down my cheeks as Ewan leaned forward and kissed me soundly on the mouth before he leaned back, a frown on his face. "You know, I had a plan."

I frowned up at him, wondering why he didn't look too happy. Had I done it wrong? Was I supposed to say yes in a different way? "What do you mean?"

"There are damn candles all set up for later asking you to marry me. It wasn't going to be public, because I know you hate public proposals. But it was going to be *us*. I just saw you here, and I couldn't hold back anymore. I want you to be mine. As possessive and domineering as that sounds. I want you to be fucking mine."

My eyes widened before I burst out laughing. "Are you serious?"

He stood up then, pulling me with him. "Amelia, come on over!"

My daughter ran toward us, her face bright. She leapt toward Ewan, causing my heart to stop, but he stood up and caught her, as if he had been doing this all of her life. That child of mine had no fear when it came to him. As if she trusted him to catch her always.

Considering that's how we first met, maybe it was imprinted on her.

Maybe Ewan was just that good of a man.

"Well," Ewan began, his voice grumpy as he set Amelia on his hip. "I jumped the gun."

"What gun?" my daughter asked, all innocent eyes.

Ewan winced. "It's just an expression. What I meant to say was I messed up our plan."

Amelia's face fell as she leaned into Ewan's hold. "Oh no!"

"What plan?" I asked, my heart beating a rapid staccato.

"Well, I had to ask somebody's permission to get this right after all."

I froze before tears started to fall once again. "Amelia?

"He's going to be my daddy. Right?" She lifted her chin as if she'd fight me if I said no.

Ewan leaned forward and kissed her cheek. "Your mommy said yes. So yes. I'm going to be your daddy. Your mommy is going to be my wife."

Amelia looked at me before she stuck out her bottom lip and pouted. "I was going to wear my dress. And then I was going to get down on my knees to help him ask. Because he needs help asking."

I hadn't realized my family had surrounded us until my father and brother burst out laughing and my mother started crying in earnest.

Ewan let out a breath. "You can still wear your dress and I'm sorry I didn't let you ask the question. So, what do you say, Amelia. Do you want to ask your mommy now?"

Amelia turned to me, wiping tears from those chubby cheeks.

"Will you marry us, Mommy? I want Ewan to be my daddy."

"Well, damn," my father muttered, and I looked to see him wiping tears. "Don't look at me. Go look at your daughter who is way too cute."

My mother was now wiping away my brother's tears and I knew I had the best family in the world.

"Don't keep the man waiting," John ordered, and I stood up, running down the final two steps before I threw myself at the two of them. I clung to Ewan's side, because I knew he would always catch me, and I leaned forward to kiss my daughter on her other cheek.

"Yes. I'll marry the both of you. I'm sorry you didn't get to wear your dress first though."

"It's okay," Amelia said solemnly before patting my cheek. "I'll get to wear another dress for the wedding too. Because I'm a flower girl," she announced very haughtily.

Ewan shook his head and laughed. "I think I'm in trouble."

"You took my daughter across state lines, and you're marrying a Montgomery. Of course you're in trouble."

"Dad," I said with a sigh, but I couldn't help but

smile at my family, wondering exactly how I got here.

It was only supposed to be a fake date, a favor for a man who'd saved my daughter. A favor that hadn't truly equated to what he had done for me.

And yet we stood on Ewan's family's land, and as his brothers, sister, and parents came riding toward us, I sighed into the arms of the man that I loved. Clover Lake had become our home, a part of me I hadn't expected. And Ewan's family had welcomed us with open arms. I knew they had so much more to give, so much more to see, and I couldn't wait to be part of it with them.

I had no idea what would happen next, no idea how I was going to face any changes that came along the way. But I knew I would be able to do it alongside the man I loved, my fake date—and the daughter who had taken his heart at first sight.

"I love you, Livvy," he whispered as he kissed me softly, and Amelia clapped her hands in his arms.

"I love you too. And I'm really sorry because I have a feeling this wedding is going to be big."

"Anything you want. You deserve it, Livvy. This flashiest, most ridiculous, most extravagant wedding you want."

"Well, there you've done it," my dad said with a laugh, and I shook my head, taking a step back.

I had fallen for a cowboy, and now the Montgomerys would be taking over Wyoming.

I couldn't wait.

Don't worry, Ewan's secretive family are each getting their own romance in the Clover Lake series. Make sure you're signed up for preorder alerts for when the next book is announced! Yay!

Shep & Shae's romance, Ink Inspired, started it all. So don't miss out Livvy's parents fell in love in New Orleans!

Lexington Montgomery finds his match in Last Chance Seduction in the Montgomery Ink Legacy series! Livvy and Ewan are also part of that series and will make guest appearances.

a note from carrie ann ryan

Thank you so much for reading **Always a Fake Bridesmaid!**

When I originally decided to write the Montgomery Ink Legacy series, I knew there would be certain Montgomerys that wanted to jump the line and get their stories first. Livvy was one of those characters. I just loved her so much and knew I needed to fit in a romance for her somewhere. Always a Fake Bridesmaid was originally supposed to be a novella in the MIL series, but then I met Ewan.

cue swooning

As soon as I figured out his backstory and ended up doing WAY too much research for a single line of dialogue and couldn't help but fall in love with a new setting and new family. I did not have time for a new series, but then again, the characters do what they want.

So welcome to Clover Lake. A brand new series of tasty romances about the McBrides. And I can't wait for you to meet Ewan's siblings in truth!

Don't worry, Ewan's secretive family are each getting their own romance in the Clover Lake series. Make sure you're signed up for preorder alerts for when the next book is announced! Yay!

Shep & Shae's romance, Ink Inspired, started it all. So don't miss out Livvy's parents fell in love in New Orleans!

Lexington Montgomery finds his match in Last Chance Seduction in the Montgomery Ink Legacy series! Livvy and Ewan are also part of that series and will make guest appearances.

If you want to make sure you know what's coming next from me, you can sign up for my newsletter at www.CarrieAnnRyan.com; follow me on twitter at

@CarrieAnnRyan, or like my Facebook page. I also have a Facebook Fan Club where we have trivia, chats, and other goodies. You guys are the reason I get to do what I do and I thank you.

Make sure you're signed up for my MAILING LIST so you can know when the next releases are available as well as find giveaways and FREE READS.

Happy Reading!

also from carrie ann ryan

The Montgomery Ink Legacy Series:
Book 1: Bittersweet Promises (Leif & Brooke)
Book 2: At First Meet (Nick & Lake)
Book 2.5: Happily Ever Never (May & Leo)
Book 3: Longtime Crush (Sebastian & Raven)
Book 4: Best Friend Temptation (Noah, Ford, and Greer)
Book 4.5: Happily Ever Maybe (Jennifer & Gus)
Book 5: Last First Kiss (Daisy & Hugh)
Book 6: His Second Chance (Kane & Phoebe)
Book 7: One Night with You (Kingston & Claire)
Book 8: Accidentally Forever (Crew & Aria)
Book 9: Last Chance Seduction (Lexington & Mercy)

ALSO FROM CARRIE ANN RYAN

The Wilder Brothers Series:
Book 1: One Way Back to Me (Eli & Alexis)
Book 2: Always the One for Me (Evan & Kendall)
Book 3: The Path to You (Everett & Bethany)
Book 4: Coming Home for Us (Elijah & Maddie)
Book 5: Stay Here With Me (East & Lark)
Book 6: Finding the Road to Us (Elliot, Trace, and Sidney)
Book 7: Moments for You (Ridge & Aurora)
Book 7.5: A Wilder Wedding (Amos & Naomi)
Book 8: Forever For Us (Wyatt & Ava)
Book 9: Pieces of Me (Gabriel & Briar)
Book 10: Endlessly Yours (Brooks & Rory)

The Cage Family
Book 1: The Forever Rule (Aston & Blakely)
Book 2: An Unexpected Everything (Isabella & Weston)
Book 3: If You Were Mine (Dorian & Harper)

Clover Lake
Book 1: Always a Fake Bridesmaid (Livvy & Ewan)

The First Time Series:
Book 1: Good Time Boyfriend (Heath & Devney)

Book 2: Last Minute Fiancé (Luca & Addison)

Book 3: Second Chance Husband (August & Paisley)

Montgomery Ink Denver:

Book 0.5: Ink Inspired (Shep & Shea)

Book 0.6: Ink Reunited (Sassy, Rare, and Ian)

Book 1: Delicate Ink (Austin & Sierra)

Book 1.5: Forever Ink (Callie & Morgan)

Book 2: Tempting Boundaries (Decker and Miranda)

Book 3: Harder than Words (Meghan & Luc)

Book 3.5: Finally Found You (Mason & Presley)

Book 4: Written in Ink (Griffin & Autumn)

Book 4.5: Hidden Ink (Hailey & Sloane)

Book 5: Ink Enduring (Maya, Jake, and Border)

Book 6: Ink Exposed (Alex & Tabby)

Book 6.5: Adoring Ink (Holly & Brody)

Book 6.6: Love, Honor, & Ink (Arianna & Harper)

Book 7: Inked Expressions (Storm & Everly)

Book 7.3: Dropout (Grayson & Kate)

Book 7.5: Executive Ink (Jax & Ashlynn)

Book 8: Inked Memories (Wes & Jillian)

Book 8.5: Inked Nights (Derek & Olivia)

Book 8.7: Second Chance Ink (Brandon & Lauren)

Book 8.5: Montgomery Midnight Kisses (Alex & Tabby Bonus(

Bonus: Inked Kingdom (Stone & Sarina)

Montgomery Ink: Colorado Springs
Book 1: Fallen Ink (Adrienne & Mace)
Book 2: Restless Ink (Thea & Dimitri)
Book 2.5: Ashes to Ink (Abby & Ryan)
Book 3: Jagged Ink (Roxie & Carter)
Book 3.5: Ink by Numbers (Landon & Kaylee)

The Montgomery Ink: Boulder Series:
Book 1: Wrapped in Ink (Liam & Arden)
Book 2: Sated in Ink (Ethan, Lincoln, and Holland)
Book 3: Embraced in Ink (Bristol & Marcus)
Book 3: Moments in Ink (Zia & Meredith)
Book 4: Seduced in Ink (Aaron & Madison)
Book 4.5: Captured in Ink (Julia, Ronin, & Kincaid)
Book 4.7: Inked Fantasy (Secret ??)
Book 4.8: A Very Montgomery Christmas (The Entire Boulder Family)

The Montgomery Ink: Fort Collins Series:
Book 1: Inked Persuasion (Jacob & Annabelle)

Book 2: Inked Obsession (Beckett & Eliza)
Book 3: Inked Devotion (Benjamin & Brenna)
Book 3.5: Nothing But Ink (Clay & Riggs)
Book 4: Inked Craving (Lee & Paige)
Book 5: Inked Temptation (Archer & Killian)

The Promise Me Series:
Book 1: Forever Only Once (Cross & Hazel)
Book 2: From That Moment (Prior & Paris)
Book 3: Far From Destined (Macon & Dakota)
Book 4: From Our First (Nate & Myra)

The Whiskey and Lies Series:
Book 1: Whiskey Secrets (Dare & Kenzie)
Book 2: Whiskey Reveals (Fox & Melody)
Book 3: Whiskey Undone (Loch & Ainsley)

The Gallagher Brothers Series:
Book 1: Love Restored (Graham & Blake)
Book 2: Passion Restored (Owen & Liz)
Book 3: Hope Restored (Murphy & Tessa)

The Less Than Series:
Book 1: Breathless With Her (Devin & Erin)
Book 2: Reckless With You (Tucker & Amelia)
Book 3: Shameless With Him (Caleb & Zoey)

ALSO FROM CARRIE ANN RYAN

The Fractured Connections Series:

Book 1: Breaking Without You (Cameron & Violet)

Book 2: Shouldn't Have You (Brendon & Harmony)

Book 3: Falling With You (Aiden & Sienna)

Book 4: Taken With You (Beckham & Meadow)

The On My Own Series:

Book 0.5: My First Glance

Book 1: My One Night (Dillon & Elise)

Book 2: My Rebound (Pacey & Mackenzie)

Book 3: My Next Play (Miles & Nessa)

Book 4: My Bad Decisions (Tanner & Natalie)

The Ravenwood Coven Series:

Book 1: Dawn Unearthed

Book 2: Dusk Unveiled

Book 3: Evernight Unleashed

The Aspen Pack Series:

Book 1: Etched in Honor

Book 2: Hunted in Darkness

Book 3: Mated in Chaos

Book 4: Harbored in Silence

Book 5: Marked in Flames

ALSO FROM CARRIE ANN RYAN

The Talon Pack:
Book 1: Tattered Loyalties
Book 2: An Alpha's Choice
Book 3: Mated in Mist
Book 4: Wolf Betrayed
Book 5: Fractured Silence
Book 6: Destiny Disgraced
Book 7: Eternal Mourning
Book 8: Strength Enduring
Book 9: Forever Broken
Book 10: Mated in Darkness
Book 11: Fated in Winter

Redwood Pack Series:
Book 1: An Alpha's Path
Book 2: A Taste for a Mate
Book 3: Trinity Bound
Book 3.5: A Night Away
Book 4: Enforcer's Redemption
Book 4.5: Blurred Expectations
Book 4.7: Forgiveness
Book 5: Shattered Emotions
Book 6: Hidden Destiny
Book 6.5: A Beta's Haven
Book 7: Fighting Fate
Book 7.5: Loving the Omega

ALSO FROM CARRIE ANN RYAN

Book 7.7: The Hunted Heart
Book 8: Wicked Wolf

The Elements of Five Series:
Book 1: From Breath and Ruin
Book 2: From Flame and Ash
Book 3: From Spirit and Binding
Book 4: From Shadow and Silence

Dante's Circle Series:
Book 1: Dust of My Wings
Book 2: Her Warriors' Three Wishes
Book 3: An Unlucky Moon
Book 3.5: His Choice
Book 4: Tangled Innocence
Book 5: Fierce Enchantment
Book 6: An Immortal's Song
Book 7: Prowled Darkness
Book 8: Dante's Circle Reborn

Holiday, Montana Series:
Book 1: Charmed Spirits
Book 2: Santa's Executive
Book 3: Finding Abigail
Book 4: Her Lucky Love
Book 5: Dreams of Ivory

ALSO FROM CARRIE ANN RYAN

The Branded Pack Series:
(Written with Alexandra Ivy)
Book 1: <u>Stolen and Forgiven</u>
Book 2: <u>Abandoned and Unseen</u>
Book 3: <u>Buried and Shadowed</u>

acknowledgments

With every book comes a new way to say thank you to those I adore the most. I couldn't do this without my team and they know it.

So thank you Team Carrie Ann for being here. You know who you are. I literally couldn't not write these books and find these characters without you.

And thank you dear reader, for still being here after all this time.

xoxo,
   Carrie Ann

praise for carrie ann ryan

"Count on Carrie Ann Ryan for emotional, sexy, character driven stories that capture your heart!" – Carly Phillips, NY Times bestselling author

"Carrie Ann Ryan's romances are my newest addiction! The emotion in her books captures me from the very beginning. The hope and healing hold me close until the end. These love stories will simply sweep you away." ~ NYT Bestselling Author Deveny Perry

"Carrie Ann Ryan writes the perfect balance of sweet and heat ensuring every story feeds the soul." - Audrey Carlan, #1 New York Times Bestselling Author

"Carrie Ann Ryan never fails to draw readers in with passion, raw sensuality, and characters that pop off the page. Any book by Carrie Ann is an absolute treat." – New York Times Bestselling Author J. Kenner

"Carrie Ann Ryan knows how to pull your heartstrings and make your pulse pound! Her wonderful Redwood Pack series will draw you in and keep you reading long into the night. I can't wait to see what comes next with the new generation, the Talons. Keep them coming, Carrie Ann!" –Lara Adrian, New York Times bestselling author of CRAVE THE NIGHT

"With snarky humor, sizzling love scenes, and brilliant, imaginative worldbuilding, The Dante's Circle series reads as if Carrie Ann Ryan peeked at my personal wish list!" - NYT Bestselling Author, Larissa Ione

"Carrie Ann Ryan writes sexy shifters in a world full of passionate happily-ever-afters." - *New York Times* Bestselling Author Vivian Arend

"Carrie Ann's books are sexy with characters you can't help but love from page one. They are heat and heart blended to perfection." *New York Times* Bestselling Author Jayne Rylon

Carrie Ann Ryan's books are wickedly funny and deliciously hot, with plenty of twists to keep you guessing. They'll keep you up all night!" USA Today Bestselling Author Cari Quinn

"Once again, Carrie Ann Ryan knocks the Dante's Circle series out of the park. The queen of hot, sexy, enthralling paranormal romance, Carrie Ann is an author not to miss!" *New York Times* bestselling Author Marie Harte

about the author

Carrie Ann Ryan is the New York Times and USA Today bestselling author of contemporary, paranormal, and young adult romance. Her works include the Montgomery Ink, Redwood Pack, Fractured Connections, and Elements of Five series, which have sold over 3.0 million books worldwide. She started writing while in graduate school for her advanced degree in chemistry and hasn't stopped since. Carrie Ann has written over seventy-five novels and novellas with more in the works. When she's not losing herself in her emotional and action-packed worlds, she's reading as much as she can while wrangling her clowder of cats who have more followers than she does.

www.CarrieAnnRyan.com

www.ingramcontent.com/pod-product-compliance
Lightning Source LLC
Chambersburg PA
CBHW010007101025
33836CB00044B/1341